They Call Me Trep

Bob Spurlock

BookLocker
Saint Petersburg, Florida

Copyright © 2020 Bob Spurlock

Print ISBN: 978-1-64719-039-2
Epub ISBN: 978-1-64719-040-8
Mobi ISBN: 978-1-64719-041-5

All rights reserved. No part of this publication may be reproduced, stored in a retrieval system, or transmitted in any form or by any means, electronic, mechanical, recording or otherwise, without the prior written permission of the author.

Published by BookLocker.com, Inc., St. Petersburg, Florida.

Printed on acid-free paper.

BookLocker.com, Inc.
2020

First Edition

Library of Congress Cataloging in Publication Data
Spurlock, Bob
They Call Me Trep by Bob Spurlock
Library of Congress Control Number: 2020919268

OVERTURE

"Beyond those monuments to heroism is the Potomac River, and on the far shore the sloping hills of Arlington National Cemetery with its row on row of simple white markers bearing crosses or Stars of David. They add up to only a tiny fraction of the price that has been paid for our freedom.

Each one of those markers is a monument to the kinds of hero I spoke of earlier. Their lives ended in places called Belleau Wood, The Argonne, Omaha Beach, Salerno and halfway around the world on Guadalcanal, Tarawa, Pork Chop Hill, the Chosin Reservoir, and in a hundred rice paddies and jungles of a place called Vietnam.

Under one such marker lies a young man--Martin Treptow--who left his job in a small-town barber shop in 1917 to go to France with the famed Rainbow Division. There, on the western front, he was killed trying to carry a message between battalions under heavy artillery fire.

We are told that on his body was found a diary. On the flyleaf under the heading, "My Pledge," he had written these words: "America must win this war. Therefore, I will work, I will save, I will sacrifice, I will endure, I will fight cheerfully and do my utmost, as if the issue of the whole struggle depended on me alone."

The crisis we are facing today does not require of us the kind of sacrifice that Martin Treptow and so many thousands of others were called upon to make. It does require, however, our best effort, and our willingness to believe in ourselves and to believe in our capacity to perform great deeds; to believe that together, with God's help, we can and will resolve the problems which now confront us.

And, after all, why shouldn't we believe that? We are Americans. God bless you, and thank you."

First Inaugural Address of President Ronald Reagan

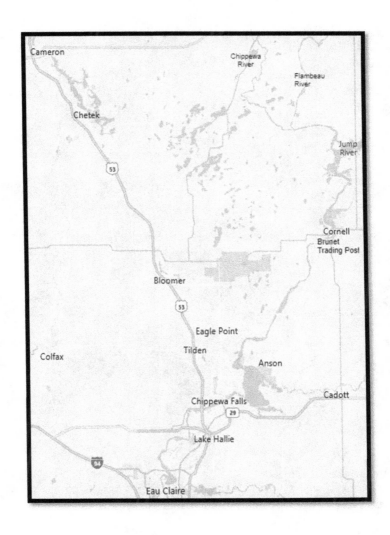

ACKNOWLEDGEMENTS

I'll start by thanking Scott Roen for allowing me to view Martin's journals. His kindness made this book possible. Many other folks helped make my research a thoroughly enjoyable journey. Sam Kooiker, Mick Samsel, Linda Burkhart and everyone at the Sanford Museum in Cherokee; archivists at the Marshfield Historical Society and the *Musee de la Grande Guerre*; 168th researcher Darrek Orwig; Hubert Caloud, Superintendent of the Oise-Aisne American Cemetery; and Ken Khachagian, President Reagan's speech writer. Thank you to Jess, my hard working secretary who accepted every draft with never a raised eyebrow, David, the very patient IT guru, Eric Bogle, who wrote the haunting *Green Fields of France,* and graciously allowed me to quote his lyrics, and the friendly folks at **greatwar.co.uk** for their map assistance (Check out their awesome website!).

Thank you, thank you! to Erica, Tami, and Diane, my editing team; to Abigail, for not letting me get discouraged, to Tami, for listening so patiently to all my changes in direction, and finally, to Jennifer for saying Why Not?; and to Andrew, for telling me I could write a book.

PROLOGUE

Josie watched the young Ojibwa effortlessly maneuver his canoe through the rapids to the riverbank. His lean body countered every tip of the small craft, and barely discernable twists of the paddle controlled each yaw around the boulders and past the whirlpools. In her thirteen years, Josephine Gauthier had encountered many visitors at her home on the river. Her French Canadian father, Francois, met the owner of their trading post many years before in Prairie du Chien. He came up the Mississippi with him, to a falls just south of the confluence of the Flambeau and Chippewa Rivers. Gauthier's boss was hired to scout a location and build a sawmill. The enterprise failed, but the scout and his new partner stayed on, disinclined to return to what passed for civilization in the Wisconsin Territory.

The men built the trading post on the western shore. For travelers following the old Indian trail along the west bank, the natural pond below the falls provided deep water, even in late summer, to ferry men and horses to the other side.

In 1846, Francois married Sophie Jandron, a Metis from Odanah, a village near Lake Superior. They raised five children at the trading post, and the second oldest was Josephine. Before she was 10, Josie could pole or paddle a birchbark canoe as well as any Ojibwe, and she was fluent in their language. French was the lingua franca, but she also learned English from the increasingly frequent visitors coming upriver.

Josie learned early to make durable moccasins and buckskin mittens. She harvested blueberries and wild plums and mastered the art of barter. The previous summer yielded a record harvest of wild fruit, and whenever Indian boys came downriver to trade, Josie would return home dropping beads. One day her father's partner gave her an inscribed silver box –from *"le vieux pays"* -- he said, "The old country", to hold her bounty. She filled it a dozen times before the first frost.

The river was the Chippewa, borne of two creeks in far northern Wisconsin. It meanders 175 miles, drains a watershed of over 10,000 square miles, and is a primary tributary of the upper Mississippi. The river was explored in 1680 by Louis Hennepin, who called the river the *Secours*, perhaps a reference to the friendly Indians, or a tribute to the Virgin Mary.

The river descends more than 500 feet from its headwaters to the Mississippi, and the various falls provided natural sites for trading posts, and eventually dams and towns. The falls below where the Flambeau and Jump emptied into the Chippewa would come to be called Brunet, after Jean Brunet, the scout who stayed on.

Mr. Brunet once told Josie that Wisconsin was a big juicy apple, and all the white men, the missionaries from Fort Howard, the iron miners below Prairie du Chien, the ones they called the badgers, and everyone else were worms headed to the core. Josie asked "What about the Indians. Who are they?" and Mr. Brunet told her they were the seeds, and the white men were spitting them out.

In the northwest, the worms came up the Chippewa, and down from Lake Superior. In the late 1600's, French fur traders built an outpost at La Pointe, on an island near the south shore of the great lake. The island is the traditional birthplace of the Ojibwe people. Thus began a century of trading, fraternization, and intermarriage between the Ojibwe and the French Canadians. A Metis from Ste. Sainte Marie, Michel Cadotte, built a larger trading post on the island, and working for the British in the first decade of the 19th Century, established trading connections along the Chippewa.

Other newcomers came for the land. Mexican War veterans were given federal acreage for their service. Northern European immigrants came to farm the rich soil immediately below the reach of the last glacier. These lands, just below the coniferous forests were "brush prairies", not true grasslands, but largely free of the hundred centuries of acidic soil that underlay the great pines.

Others, who had settled earlier near the growing cities along Lake Michigan, saved their money and bought land in the Chippewa Valley. One was a German immigrant named Martin Treptow. He'd traveled from Germany to Kenosha in the 1860s, and later purchased 80 acres of farmland two miles west of the Chippewa River. His son, Albert, married a local girl, and found work with Frederick Weyerhaeuser's lumber company. On January 19, 1894, the third of their five children, to be named after his grandfather, was born in Chippewa Falls.

The Treptow farm 2019. The barn walls are original.
Courtesy of Hernandez Photography

St. John's confirmation class, 1904. Martin Treptow is believed to be first row, second from right. *Courtesy of St. John's Lutheran Church.*

St. John's Lutheran Church, 2019. Eagle Point, Wisconsin. *Courtesy of Hernandez Photography.*

Chapter One

The Child's faith is new

Whole – like his principle

Wide- like the Sunrise

On fresh eyes

Never had a doubt

The Child's Faith is New Emily Dickinson

Martin Treptow began the final day of the nineteenth century attending to chores safely assignable to a five-year-old. When he finished, he washed up and changed while his father hitched the team. The weather was mild for late December, and Albert suggested they take the wagon into Chippewa Falls to attend services, rather than just heading up the road to St. John's where they usually spent Sunday mornings. After church, the family enjoyed a New Year's Eve meal in town.

The big mill at the falls was quiet, awaiting the spring thaw and a river filled with winter-cut logs. Each year brought fewer of the giant white and Norway pine, and more hemlock. Albert didn't need to return to the woods to know the logging era was ending. Young Martin, of course, couldn't distinguish birch from oak, and told his father he wanted to be a lumberjack when he grew up. On summer evenings, after chores, Martin would head north across the field and listen to stories told by Frank

Ermatinger, who owned the adjoining farm. Frank's father, James, married the daughter of Michel Cadotte, and built the trading post near the town that now bore his name. His son shared with young Martin the stories he'd learned as a child -- and a few he invented over the years. Martin was fascinated with the tales of the river and the legendary lumbermen. For Albert, who'd spent winters in the woods, the trade held no romance, only hard work and constant danger. Albert hoped it would be years before he needed to tell his young son anything other than "We shall see."

Albert always hoped Martin would stay on the farm and someday inherit the land, just as he had after his own father's fatal accident. Previous years had yielded good harvests, and when the Eagleton creamery opened in 1901, Albert expanded into dairying. Young Martin didn't shy from hard work, and he enjoyed life in the country. In the summer he fished O'Neil Creek and swam in Popple Lake, a half mile to the east. In the winter he skated the lake with his brothers and sisters or went sledding on the hill across the road from the farm. But he knew early on the agrarian life was not for him. When Martin was ten, he again told his parents he wanted to work in the "big timber" like his father. Albert tried to explain that now, in 1904; there was no more "big timber" to be cut. Had Martin been older, he'd have noticed far fewer young men in Chippewa Falls on weekends, and the sharp decline in the number of working girls.

Economic explanations were lost on the boy, however, and almost out of ideas, Albert began to share with his son stories of horrific injuries in lumber country. He told the boy of lost arms, drownings, deglovings, decapitations, and all manner of mayhem suffered by those foolish enough to seek adventure in the woods. He told Martin the story of Joseph Dugal, a young man from Chippewa Falls, who was replacing giant reinforcement beams under a bridge. Dugal fixed one of the heavy beams into a temporary slot then bent down to wench the next beam into place. Just then, the end bearing gave way on the upper beam, and it swung down and caught Dugal squarely in the head. Albert made sure to quote for his son the newspaper's description "crushed into a shapeless mass." The story gave Martin nightmares but failed to quell his desire to work in the woods.

Martin was now attending the country school a quarter mile from the farm and was an excellent student. He learned to read early on and consumed every book he could find. He particularly enjoyed stories of Europe, whether they involved Roman legions, knights in shining armor, or the modern states. He read, and his class discussed, the Entente Cordiale of 1904, which ended a millennium of rivalry between Great Britain and France. Neither the boy, nor for that matter, anyone else in the world, appreciated at the time that the treaty effectively sealed the fate of three quarters of a million young Englishmen.

In 1905, something finally convinced Martin of the dangers of lumbering. Late on July 6th, a huge log jam developed just below the Little Falls dam near Holcombe. When the word went out, seventy Chippewa Lumber and Boom men boarded the Omaha train early Friday in Chippewa Falls and headed north. In midsummer, the lumberjacks were less busy, and many of the men had spent the previous night, and the early morning, in the taverns. Some were still dressed from the night before. Arriving at the dam, they overloaded a bateau, which almost immediately capsized in the rapids below the dam. Eleven of the sixteen never came out of the river. The next day, Albert and Martin joined volunteers to search for their bodies. One of the men, Ole Horne, lived in Chippewa Falls and was famous throughout the pineries as "Whitewater Ole" who could dance a jig on a log and break up the biggest jam. His body floated downriver and was found tangled in debris on July 12th. Shortly after that Martin asked his father if he might get him a job at Burt Mason's new shoe factory in Chippewa Falls.

So in the late spring of 1906, after the crops were planted and the school year ended, Martin began his first career, as a factory cobbler. Even for a 12-year-old, for whom everything was new, the tasks could be mastered quickly, and the job soon proved tedious. Martin needed an outlet for his creative talents and a muse for his intellectual curiosity. Fortunately, several years earlier, members of the city's Progressive League convinced Andrew Carnegie to contribute $20,000 to build a city library. Martin became a frequent visitor, and read whatever he could, whenever he could. He also began writing letters. The train made three daily runs between Chippewa Falls and points north. Martin could catch the afternoon train to Eagle Point, walk the mile or so to the farm for supper, and return to Chippewa Falls by sundown. His parents thought it odd at first that Martin wrote them letters, since he always saw them in person before the letters arrived. When they pointed that out to their son, Martin explained that he just enjoyed writing, and a letter to them guaranteed an audience.

The Treptow home 2019. Bloomer, Wisconsin.
Photograph property of the author.

Chapter Two

I must to the barber's, monsieur, for methinks I am marvelous

hairy about the face.

William Shakespeare

A Midsummer Night's Dream. Act 4, scene 1

By 1911, Martin knew his future didn't lie in Chippewa Falls. With the mill closing and the lumbermen gone, other enterprises shut down or relocated, and the city fathers scrambled to entice other business. Chippewa Falls had been awarded the Home for the Feeble-Minded in 1865 by the Wisconsin legislature, but the facility was considerably smaller than similar hospitals in Michigan or Iowa and offered far fewer jobs. So that summer, 17-year-old Martin Treptow boarded the train to Minneapolis, to attend barber college.

It was a time of change for the entire family. Having saved enough money, Albert decided it was time to move to town, where the roads were better, the electricity reliable, and the plumbing indoors. Albert shared his son's concerns about the future of Chippewa Falls, and he had no desire to move all the way to Eau Claire. So that summer, the family began building a home 7 miles north, in the village of Bloomer.

Chippewa County was much smaller by then. Not only geographically, when the state partitioned the northern section into a new county, but by the march of progress. By 1902, a railroad line ran from Chippewa Falls, at the south end of the county, to its new northeast boundary in Holcombe. In 1909, a self-powered streetcar made two daily runs between Stanley and Jump River, some 35 miles to the north.

Several years before, the first automobiles appeared in the area. In 1906, A.T. Newman drove a car to his hometown of Bloomer. Local residents got wind of the great event, and he was met at the edge of town with a band and an impromptu parade. Newman was promptly arrested for disturbing the peace and sentenced to buy everyone a cigar.

Technology also was changing lives in the home and the workplace. The Bloomer Telephone Company was formed in 1902, and that same year, Bloomer Power and Light brought electrical service to the town. As the village modernized, the business district moved away from the flood prone creek below the mill dam to the long street running to the new Catholic Church to the north.

In 1904, the new Bloomer high school graduated its first formal class. Albert had no luck convincing his son to receive a secondary diploma, but Martin did return to Bloomer from Minneapolis. He enjoyed the fact that he could walk to the soda fountain or the theater, and he was happy to discover their new home was only a stone's throw away from Duncan Creek, where he could fish or swim. In the winter, he'd take his little brother, Clarence up Bluff Street to sled down Werner's Hill. He didn't mind walking slowly to let Clarence keep up if it gave Martin a chance to tip his hat to the pretty, dark-eyed teenage girl who lived at the other end of the block from the Norwegian church.

The Treptows were hardly destitute. They could afford to hire a farm hand while building their new home. However, the construction depleted their savings and denied Martin the luxury of finding his way in the world through his parents' largesse. In the summer of 1913, he saw an ad posted in Werner's General Store seeking workers to expand the Soo Line Railroad near Cameron, in Barron County to the north.If he found affordable boarding, he could manage a small weekly savings. His parents gave their approval, and Martin's father arranged a ride from Bloomer to Rice Lake in the back of a delivery truck running a regular route north from Chippewa Falls. On the morning of June 30, 2013, Martin stepped in the back of the Ford Model T C cab heading for Cameron.

Martin was surprised to find he was not the only human cargo that day. Seated across from him in the cramped rear compartment was a smiling young man, holding, of all things, a football. He extended a hand.

"The name's Charles. Folks call me Gus."

"Martin Treptow. People call me Trep. Where you're going with that football?"

"I'm going to work on a railroad gang. I can use the money."

"I guess we're headed to the same place," Martin responded, "But why'd you bring a football?"

"I play football in college, and I like to practice throwing it."

"It must be a pretty small college. You don't look more than five foot six, and I bet you don't weigh 150 lbs. And why do you want to practice throwing? I don't play football, but I know you run with the ball to score."

Gus smiled. "Running is old stuff. I threw it last year, and the year before that, and we always took the other team by surprise. This year I plan to do it as much as coach allows."

"Why are you going to work on a railroad gang? I thought college men took it easy during the summer.

Gus smiled again. "I'm from Chippewa, Trep. My dad's dead, and my mother takes in laundry. So every summer I find work. For the last month I've been a lifeguard. Now there's a job for you. Plenty of girls, plenty of sun, plenty of time to throw the football, and a long swim whenever you feel like it."

"So why are you here?"

"I came back to see my parents. Tuesday is my birthday. And I need to get in shape before next season. So why are you heading to Cameron? A few years ago I played base ball with some of you strapping Bloomer lads. I mean no disrespect, but isn't farming more suited to you?"

"My father's a farmer, but I want to work for myself."

The truck was nearing New Auburn, and everywhere the men looked was fresh cutaway land. "Then buy some land up here and start your own farm," Gus suggested.

"You're not a farmer, are you, Gus? Those stumps are what are left of 10,000 years of white pine. The land's acidic. The Norwegians brought here by the lumber companies don't know that yet, but they'll find out."

Gus had no more questions for Martin, and before long, both young men were dozing on their bags.

It was almost noon when the truck pulled into Chetek, 10 miles north of New Auburn.

"I'll be stopping for lunch," the driver told the boys, "You're welcome to get yourself something to eat or just wait for me." Neither Gus nor Martin had eaten since early morning, and both had enough money with them to buy lunch. They accompanied the driver into the Pine Ridge Café and took a table next to an old couple. The man scarcely noticed the boys, but the woman eyed them with interest. Martin guessed her to be in her 60s and thought she might be part Indian. She was reading the *Chetek Alert*, and she folded the paper and greeted the boys.

"Well, well, what fine young men. Tell me, why are you not in the fields?"

Gus spoke first. "We're going to Cameron to work on the railroad."

The woman smiled. "Well, maybe I'll join you."

"No offense, ma'am but I don't think even a woman in the.... um.... prime of her life could do the work we'll be doing."

"Why you impertinent little shit! How do you know I'm not in the prime of my life right now? And men's work, is it? I'll have you know, young man, that I paddled a birchbark canoe over the Brunet Falls before I was 10. I've driven oxen, I've felled trees wider than you are tall –which ain't saying much - and I've cleared fields. I may be an old woman now, but when I was young, I could do anything a man could do." She caught herself. "Except vote."

Gus had never been called an "impertinent little shit" before, but he'd been called much worse at Forbes Field the previous fall, and he quickly recovered his bravado. "So you're a suffragist, too? What do women know about the world? What do women know about business?"

"Little man, I can point out your obvious…" she paused for effect, "shortcomings in three languages. I watched Ezra Cornell map out plans for his university. And I was doing business with the Indians before your parents were born."

Gus bristled at the comment on his height, but said nothing.

"She looked at Gus for a long moment. "You don't look like a laborer. You look like a college boy."

"I am. I'm visiting my mother in Chippewa. And I don't like being idle."

"Well, perhaps you have a redeeming quality after all."

"Girls my age say I have many redeeming qualities."

"Girls your age are easily fooled." The old woman then turned to Martin.

"And who might you be, young man?"

"My name is Martin Treptow. They call me Trep."

"What are your views on the suffrage, Trep?"

"Well, ma'am, I'm afraid I haven't thought much about it."

She looked intently at Martin. "Fair enough. Men never have thought much about it. Say, do you have a cigarette?"

Martin's eyes widened. He liked to consider himself somewhat worldly, having been to Minneapolis. Still, he'd never had a woman ask him for a cigarette, and he fumbled in his shirt pocket. "Uh, here you go, ma'am."

"I really don't want a cigarette, Trep. I was curious to see how you'd respond. One day a young lady is going to come along and expect you to have an opinion about the suffrage, and when she asks you for a cigarette, she'll be watching to see how you handle yourself."

She reached across the table and drew something from her bag. "Young man, I'm going to give you something to properly hold your cigarettes. When that young lady asks, you impress her with this little case. This was given to me by Jean Brunet himself, and I stored beads in it when I was a child. I've carried it all these years."

It was a small silver box, approximately four inches long, with a clasp on the side, and a French inscription on the ornate cover. It could hold perhaps half a dozen cigarettes and wooden matches.

"Mr. Brunet told me it came from France, and when he gave it to me, he said he no longer had use for it. Now I no longer have use for it. Store your cigarettes properly and impress a young lady someday."

"Are you sure? Gosh, thank you, ma'am. If you don't mind my asking, I didn't catch your name."

"My name is Josephine Robert. Now you boys enjoy your lunch, and work hard on that railroad. And Mr. Martin Treptow, when that little fart needs help, you be sure to lend him a hand."

She winked at Gus, and he forced a smile.

Chapter Three

The summer of 2013 was unusually warm and dry, and the gang very quickly came to appreciate the seriousness of their task. The Soo Line track was to be reinforced from Ladysmith west to Cameron and beyond. Yard by yard, the track was lifted, the railbed widened and reinforced, and new ties laid. The day started at first light, and barring heavy rains, continued until the sun finally became more generous with its shadows.

The crew was a diverse collection of strong backs: two college boys from the University of Minnesota, three young Ojibwa, two teenagers from Rice Lake, a local boy from Cameron, and a half dozen middle aged railroad men who look sixty, and worked like they were eighty. Gus was not the strongest of the group, but Martin was soon impressed with his energy. He was tireless and relentlessly competitive. He was always breaking the crew into teams, which to Martin's surprise, seemed to motivate everyone, even the old railroad men. Gus found the college boys insufficiently serious (he eventually confessed to Martin that he'd been rejected by the University of Minnesota), and the railroad men lazy. But Gus' enthusiasm made everyone more productive.

One day a hard summer rain allowed the crew to quit early. The Rice Lake boys invited everyone north for beers in a local tavern. The railroad men and the Ojibwa declined, but Gus, the college boys, the young fellow from Cameron, and Martin accepted the offer. By the time they reached town the skies had cleared, and the group instead bought beer and headed for the lake. The rainstorm hadn't broken the heat, and the water looked inviting. Soon several of the young men were in the water, and true to form, Gus challenged everyone to a race.

"There are seven of us, and eight beers left. Winner gets the second beer."

Everyone declined except Johnny Cook, the quiet Cameron kid.

"To the buoy and back?"

Cook nodded, Martin counted down, and the two were in the water. Gus, all flailing arms and legs, reminded Martin of a river sturgeon caught in the shallows at Jim's Falls. Cook splashed very little, and each stroke mirrored its predecessor. They rounded the buoy with Cook well in the lead, and he ultimately beat Gus by a good four body lengths.

Gus complimented the victor in his own way.

"Next time," he smiled. "I'll be ready for ya."

On the drive back to Cameron, Martin asked Gus why everything was a competition for him.

"Trep, man's a competitive animal. I bet you saw it back on the farm. If someone bought a new team, the next guy wanted a steam tractor. If somebody built a new outhouse, the neighbor would build a three-holer, and the next neighbor would install indoor plumbing.

"Here's what I've learned, Trep. You want to get something done, pit one man against another, and they'll fight to get it done first. Remember that."

One afternoon in the second week, well before quitting time, the boss unexpectedly yelled "Stand down!" The men looked at him quizzically.

"I was told that at exactly 3 PM some big bugs would be out here to look at your work. Speak to them only if spoken to, and don't cuss."

Not two minutes later, the men watched a small cloud of dust grow larger along the south side of the tracks. Martin had seen fancy cars two years before in Minneapolis, but nothing like this. And all the men on the gang, even those who had never traveled more than ten miles in their lifetime, recognized immediately that the drivers didn't own those cars; they were chauffeuring the men riding in the back. The carriages they piloted were Simplex Model 38 touring cars, among the most expensive vehicles in the world.

It happened that Martin was the only one standing when the cars pulled up to the crew. Others were sitting against trees or sprawled on the ground, but Martin had taken just that moment to stand and admire their last 10 days of work. He thought the elderly gentleman in the first vehicle looked familiar, but the name escaped him. To his surprise, the old man was the first to alight, and he strode directly up to Martin.

"You have a fine stature, young man. What is your name?"

"Martin. Martin Treptow, sir."

"And what brings you to my friend's railroad, may I ask?"

"I want to work hard and be respected, sir," Martin responded.

"Bullshit!" The word echoed through the trees, and every man on the gang jumped. The drivers were startled, apparently having never heard the old man swear. He laughed, "So you've pleased your mother. Tell her you were asked and gave an answer she would approve. Now tell me what brings you to this dusty railbed."

Martin suddenly recognized his friendly inquisitor. "Well, sir, my father worked for you, and I thought working with the railroad might help me get in the lumber business."

"The trees are gone, young man. If you want to work in the lumber business, move to Seattle."

"I don't know if I'll be moving to Seattle, sir. But I'd appreciate whatever other advice you could give me," Martin said.

The old man studied him for a moment, narrowed his eyes, and spoke slowly. "Work harder than the man next to you. Be willing to sacrifice. Approach every task as if its success depends on you alone." Then he smiled and added, "And harvest something that grows faster than trees."

"I'll try to follow that advice. Thank you, Mr. Weyerhaeuser."

Chapter Four

Gus and the University of Minnesota boys left in early August, and the Ojibwa departed soon after. The contract was completed in September, and Martin said goodbye to the remaining crew and headed back to Bloomer. He caught just the end of the potato harvest, and soon found himself with little to do. The Chicago and Northwestern made three daily runs between Bloomer and Eagle Point, and he could leave early, complete the daily chores, and be back to Bloomer by late afternoon. The village now had several soda fountains, and a movie theater, and he could easily walk wherever he wanted to go.

The proliferation of rail service meant Bloomer saw more visitors-relatives, businessmen, and just tourists looking for adventure in northern Wisconsin. Martin tried to strike up a conversation with someone whenever he traveled, and when he didn't get a chance to talk, he'd pick up a newspaper left on the seat. He enjoyed his new hometown, and liked spending time with his family. Martin happily accepted the mantle of being Clarence's big brother and best friend. Still, Martin longed for a real career. He'd applied at Dutton's Barber Shop, but there were no openings.

One afternoon, Martin walked to Kranzfelder's Meat Market to pick up a sausage and a roast his mother ordered. Business was brisk, and Martin got in line behind two local women. He overheard one say, "Can you believe it, they still haven't gotten rid of their outhouse." Martin remembered what Gus said about competition, and he got to thinking about all the new inventions he'd seen in his short lifetime. Not just aeroplanes and diesel locomotives, but things that changed ordinary people's lives - cars and electric lights and music players. As much as they improved the world, they also made folks compare themselves to each other. It seemed to Martin that not too long ago, some people were real rich, and some were real poor, but most folks were just sorta in between. Twenty years ago, everyone coming into town had shit on their shoes. Now that would betray a family's reliance on a horse and buggy. If somebody had a Victrola when their neighbor had a gramophone or if they had a telephone and their neighbors had yet to sign up, they considered themselves better. Martin wasn't sure whether this was a good thing at all.

Several days later, Martin walked to the Bloomer House for breakfast, then caught the morning train to Eagle Point. He picked up a newspaper left on one of the seats and turned to the comic pages. Martin's parents could never understand why he bothered to read cartoons; Martin couldn't understand why anyone wouldn't. On that early spring day, he noticed a new comic, entitled "Keeping Up with the Joneses." The cartoon reflected exactly what Martin had thought about two days earlier.

Chapter Five

On June 28, 1914, Austrian Archduke Franz Ferdinand was assassinated in Sarajevo, Serbia. The event initially drew scant attention in farming country, but as the story grew, it began to dominate the conversation in the taverns, the barber shops, and on the train. On July 25th, Austria Hungary severed ties with Serbia, and began to mobilize its military. Three days later, Russia, Serbia's ally, also began to mobilize. On August 1st, Austria Hungary's ally, Germany declared war on Russia, and France, Russia's ally, declared war as well. Two days later, Germany declared war on France, and on August 4th, invaded Belgium. That prompted England to declare war on Germany, and the United States Congress, reacting immediately to the crisis, declared its neutrality. By September, France and England were frantically trying to hold the Germans at the Marne River, 30 miles from Paris. That engagement spawned half a million casualties, and it was apparent the mobilizations were not feints.

Before long, Americans everywhere, even those in the far reaches of Wisconsin, grew concerned that America might be drawn into the conflict. President Wilson continued to reassure the nation that America would not be dragged into Europe's war. Still, Americans kept a wary eye on developments abroad.

In April 1915, near Ypres, in Belgium, the Germans began using chlorine gas on the battlefield, transforming what a New York schoolteacher had suggested to Secretary of War Edwin Stanton fifty-three years earlier into deadly reality. The French and English soon followed suit. On May 7th, the British passenger liner Lusitania was torpedoed by a German submarine near the coast of England. American opinion began to sway in favor of the French-Russian-English alliance, but millions of German immigrants were less enthusiastic. Many others simply saw no need to become enmeshed in a European conflict. Wilson continued to promise he'd keep the nation out of war, and Americans wanted to believe him.

Back in northern Wisconsin, August 1915 delivered the most miserable summer weather anyone could remember. The rains started the first week, and daytime temperatures barely reached the low fifties. A few fortunate farmers salvaged their second hay crop, but the corn, wheat, and potatoes were lost. The rain and cold continued, and by late August, it was apparent the growing season was a complete bust. Martin's summer farm work was largely finished, and his desire to find full time employment doing anything else was rekindled. At the end of the month, his parents gave their blessing, and Martin began scouring the ads in the local papers. He found a barber in Marshfield, 60 miles to the southeast, looking for apprentices. The next day, Martin reached the owner, Frank Dolezal by phone, and arranged a meeting for the following week.

On September 11, 1915, the same day Bulgaria began to mobilize its forces in support of the Central Powers, Martin boarded the train in Bloomer and headed to his interview. He rode the Chicago and Northwestern to Merrillan, where he boarded the Omaha line to Marshfield. Early that evening, he left the depot on South Central Avenue and checked into the Blodgett Hotel. The next morning, he dressed and shaved, and walked a block to 128 South Central Avenue, where he introduced himself to Mr. Dolezal. Thus began Martin Treptow's barbering career.

Marshfield, Wisconsin railroad depot, 1910. *Courtesy of the Marshfield Historical Society*

Chapter Six

Winter 1916

Martin figured he had about two hours of daylight left and decided if no one came into the shop in the next ten minutes, he'd close early and enjoy the January thaw. He peered out the front door, down the street toward the railroad depot, and saw no one. He turned the sign in the window to "closed" and swept up the remnants of a slow day's barbering. Not five minutes later, a well-dressed elderly gentleman poked his head around the door. "Is it too late for a shave and a haircut?" he asked.

The man stepped into the shop slowly and removed his hat. He was almost entirely bald, save for vestiges of a more hirsute past above each ear. "I'm happy to stay open for you, mister, and I'll give you a shave, but I think a haircut would be stealing. No offense, but if I miss a few hairs, who would notice?

" I would notice, young man. Your task is to make one side exactly match the other, and I'll pay you one dollar."

Martin's standard fair was 25 cents for a haircut and 10 cents for a shave. Eight bits wouldn't make up for a slow day, but it wouldn't hurt.

"Then sit yourself down, sir. What brings you to Marshfield?"

"I have speaking engagements. I spoke last night in Wausau, and in two days I'll be in Eau Claire. I've been retained to speak in your fair city this summer, in what I'm told will be the world's largest round barn," the man said.

"Oh, yes, the round barn. They're building it down on 17th Street and it'll be completed this spring. My customers tell me they plan to drive the Norwegians crazy by offering them a dollar if they can piss in a corner."

The old man laughed. "May I use that joke this summer, or will I anger the Norwegians?"

"The Norwegians have a good sense of humor, sir, but I'm afraid it's already an old joke."

"Advice taken, young man."

"Now what exactly is it you lecture about?"

The old man moved very deliberately away from the front door. If not for his steady gaze, Martin might have assumed him to be feeble minded. He stopped in front of the barber chair, turned and placed both hands on the armrests. He stepped backward gingerly and lifted himself with a grunt. He winced as he turned to look at Martin. He wasn't dressed like a laborer, and his hands weren't calloused. Martin guessed the fellow to be about 70, and figured some natural malady, rheumatism maybe, had stiffened him up.

The man ignored Martin's question while he tried to find a position that didn't make him grimace. Finally he turned, raised his chin, and for the first time smiled a little. "I give two different lectures; 'Crime Does Not Pay', and 'What Life Has Taught Me.'"

"Crime does not pay? Were you a gunfighter?" Martin asked.

"Gunfighter? That word's an invention of dime novelists. I suppose one would say I was once a shootist." the old man said.

That explained the pained movements. "You were shot!"

"Twelve times. The first time at the Battle of Little Rock in 1864 when I was barely 20. And 12 years later, I was shot 11 times". He paused and looked directly at Martin. "In Northfield."

"Northfield? You were with the James Gang?"

"I was. And I didn't dare take a drink for a year afterwards, for fear I wouldn't hold water."

Martin knew the ad lib was long practiced, but he indulged the old man a smile. He figured he was getting one line of "Crime does not pay" for free, and besides, the fellow was paying him three times the usual rate.

The old man met Martin's gaze again. "That was a long time ago, and now people pay to hear my stories."

"I'm sure they want to hear how you found the straight and narrow."

"Young fella, I could wax eloquent about passing gas and people would still come. They care not at all about what life's taught me. To them I'm the last fleeting whiff of adventure. When I travel in the south they ask about Quantrill; when I get in the Great Plains, they ask about Billy the Kid or Wild Bill Hickok, neither of whom I ever met, by the way. I tell folks adventure is where they make it. The trouble with people nowadays is they either pine for the past or waste their time dreaming about the future. Folks need to live in the present.

"I'll tell you a story. Three months ago, I was riding a train that stopped outside Kearny, Nebraska. We all got out to stretch our legs, and by God, what do we see but a herd of buffalo. Of course, they weren't wild; some farmer was raising 'em. I'm enjoying the chance to see something I'll probably never see again. I turn to say that to the fellow next to me, and he says 'I gotta run in the car and get my Kodak!' Well, of course by the time he gets back these buffalo have wandered way off, and what'd he lose? He lost his chance to live in the present.

"But hell, who am I to complain? Let folks pay to hear the wild stories of the old gunfighter. Let 'em place their hands on my scars. 'Touch me and see. A spirit does not have flesh and bones as you see I have.'"

"I don't think St. Luke was referring to a shootist."

"You know your Good Book. Very commendable. So, tell me about yourself, young barber. Are you a wealthy merchant?" the old man asked.

"I moved here six months ago. I like the people, and I like the town, but I don't think it's working out."

"It must be your boss. Is he stingy? Is he a tyrant?"

"If only he was", Martin mused. "Frank Dolezal might be the friendliest, most popular man in Marshfield. And the stories he tells – Why, he's worked in the Dakotas in the fields, and he's been a lumberjack. He hunts and fishes, and always brings in enough for me and all his neighbors."

"And your problem is…?"

"Well, most of my pay comes from the heads I cut and the faces I shave. Everyone who comes in wants to hear one of Frank's stories. The only locals who don't want Frank cutting their hair are those who don't like his politics. But he's a

Republican, like most everyone around these parts. So, I just get the Socialists, and they tend to leave their hair long."

The old man smiled again. "And what are your politics? Do you favor temperance? Where do you stand on the suffrage? Will you be voting for Wilson?" the man inquired.

"I find it safer to keep my politics to myself," Martin responded. "I enjoy a good beer, and if the vote means that women will be too busy to cut their husband's hair, I'm all for suffrage. Will I vote for Wilson? We're not at war. Although after what the Huns did to the *Lusitania,* I don't know how long we can avoid it."

"Don't believe everything you read about the *Lusitania,* young man. There's money in warfare, and I'm sure that ship was carrying munitions. And I'll bet the British could have done more than they did to protect that ship. Make no mistake; their generals want America in the war. Do you have any idea how many they lost at Ypres and Gallipoli? They need more cannon fodder, son, and before long, it will be young fellas like you in the trenches.

"But for now, my tonsorial friend, make yourself happy. Find a good woman. If there are too few hairy heads in this town, find another town. I've lectured, and I've performed with Buffalo Bill in every state of the union. I've seen every railroad town in the Middle West, and there's a thousand Marshfields.

"Put the scissors down and hand me my grip. I have newspaper clippings from places I lectured, and you're free to look and find yourself a home with more heads in need of your services. I'm at the Blodgett just up the street. Bring 'em back to me this evening."

"Thank you, sir. I'll look at them after I close up, and I'll bring them by," Martin said.

The haircut took no longer than their brief discussion, and Martin was not in the habit of soliciting conversation during a shave. Talk moves the Adam's apple, and enthusiasm causes movement of the neck, not a recommended *pas de deux* with a sharp straight razor.

When his shave was finished, the old man rose slowly from the chair, looked in the mirror and rubbed the back of his left hand against his chin and neck. "A fine performance, young man. On Friday I'll be 72, and I'll consider this my birthday shave and haircut."

Martin watched the old man move haltingly toward the door. "Can I ask you one question before you leave?"

"Certainly."

"Were you ever afraid?"

Martin clearly caught him by surprise. Apparently this was a question a thousand audiences had never posed. "Now why in heaven's name would you ask me that?"

"I was reading about Ypres. I've never faced real danger, and I don't know what I would do."

The old man said nothing for a long moment. He was staring at Martin, but his eyes were somewhere far away." One day…somewhere… you'll look and everyone around you will be shitting themselves. If you're truly a man, you'll do what they can't bring themselves to do." He turned and gazed into the sunset, then spoke again. "It's funny. Time just slows down, and it's just you. In all the noise and commotion, you're all by yourself. And when you get through it, by God, you're respected."

Then he indulged Martin a wry smile. "'Course...you might not get through it."

The old outlaw laid four quarters on the counter and ambled into the setting sun.

Martin locked the door, and finished cleaning. He picked up the stack of clippings, sat back in the barber chair and skimmed two dozen newspapers. Unfortunately, the old man generally saved only the notices of his upcoming lectures, and occasionally a review of his performance. Martin was about to put the clippings down when a page from the April 17, 1911 *Cherokee Times* caught his eye. It included an article for a lecture entitled, "What Life Has Taught Me", by Cole Younger, "The Famous Outlaw". But that wasn't what got Martin's attention. What he noticed was a small ad at the bottom of the page for "Popma's Barber Shop." The ad promised "The closest shave in Cherokee!" and finished with, "Always looking for good assistants."

COLE YOUNGER *Library of Congress*

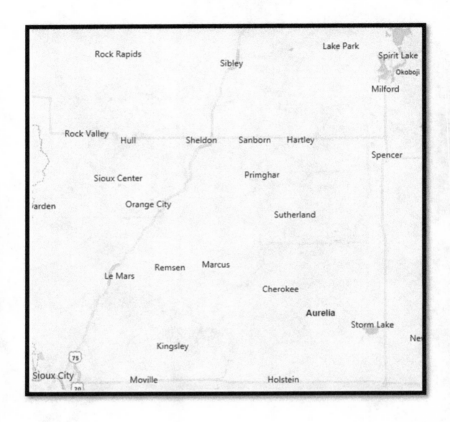

Chapter Seven

Cherokee, Iowa. July 26, 1916

The ride from Minneapolis to Sioux City was long and uneventful. The train followed the Minnesota River down to Mankato and the undulating terrain had held his interest. But the rolling hills of river and lake country had long since given way to broad, flat prairies, and as the train steamed west to the Iowa border, the unbroken horizon put him to sleep. He awoke to the sound of children behind him yelling, "We're in Iowa! Look for Hawkeye Point!" Martin rubbed his eyes and looked out the window, expecting to see a mountain, or at least some obvious natural feature. But he saw nothing more than flat fields. He asked their parents, "What's Hawkeye Point?"

"Why, it's the highest mountain in Iowa," the father responded with a smile. "Look carefully or you'll miss it."

Martin looked out again but saw nothing but a tiny gradient change near a farm.

"All I see is a bump in the field."

"That's it! That's the highest point in Iowa!" the father laughed. "One thousand six hundred seventy feet!"

Martin was hoping the man was joking. If folks really got all excited about a bump half the size of Werner's Hill, this was going to be a pretty dull place. He wasn't regretting the decision, but he'd seen higher manure piles. He mused again about what put him on this train chugging into the heartland. Truth was, he'd thought about leaving Marshfield even before Mr. Younger walked into his barber shop. The newspaper clippings just gave him some options. He hadn't bothered to write or call ahead to Mr. Popma, and he had no idea if a job would be waiting for him. Martin figured if there was no work in Cherokee, he'd head further west.

Back when they approached the Iowa border, Martin realized the train was behind schedule, and he worried he wouldn't be able to catch the Flyer on its daily run from Sioux City. He de-boarded quickly, and was relieved to see the Cherokee-bound train had just pulled in. Martin was tending to his bags when he heard someone yell "Stop the thief!" Just as he reached to grab his bag, a young Negro caught a foot on Martin's outstretched arm and went headlong off the platform. Several policemen were on the man immediately, and they thanked Martin for his assistance.

"This man robbed the barber shop in Marcus. People saw him board the train, and the station master called ahead. You've done a great service, young man."

Martin began to say that all he'd done was to try and get his bags out of the way, but he was already being congratulated by a small knot of other travelers. He smiled, shook their hands, and made his way to the next train.

The Flyer covered the 60 miles to Cherokee in just over three hours. By now, Martin was wide awake and eager to see his new hometown. He noticed the terrain was offering more variation, and also noticed the day was becoming extremely warm. In fact, the hot spell would continue for two more weeks, and take the lives of dozens of farmhands and elderly folks. It would be one of the worst heatwaves to strike western Iowa in three decades.

As he approached Cherokee, Martin's thoughts were not on the weather, but on his destination. Martin had booked a room at the Lewis and looked forward to a couple nights in a nice hotel. He arrived early, and curious to explore what might be his new home, left his bags with a porter and walked out into a hot, humid Iowa summer afternoon.

Railroad depot, Cherokee, Iowa, 1903

West Main Street, Cherokee, Iowa, 1910

Photographs courtesy of *Cherokee Historic
Preservation Commission*

Cherokee had only a few thousand inhabitants, and the hospital for the feeble minded was the only significant industry. Martin noticed, though, that the railroad depot was busy, and he thought travelers might make at least semi-frequent customers. He walked out of the depot onto 4th Street and turned right onto Main. As he walked by the American Theatre, he heard a rehearsal of some sort through the open doors. He stopped for a moment and listened to a woman singing *"America, I Love You."* She sang slowly, and her voice floated effortlessly between octaves.

Back at the country school in Eagle Point, a music teacher from Chippewa Falls would come by once a week. She had each child sing, then assigned them a range based on where their voice was most comfortable. Their *tessitura,* she called it. She christened most of the young boys "boy sopranos," until the girls laughed at them, then changed it to "high tenors" to make them feel better. Martin thought the teacher would be challenged by the voice he was hearing. It sounded comfortable in every range – soprano to contralto. Had he not been standing in the hot sun, Martin might have stayed to listen. But he was eager to get to the hotel and out of his clothes. He moved on but paused when he reached 2nd Street. There, on the southwest corner, above the stairs leading to the basement, he noticed the sign: "Popma's Barber Shop."

Martin turned back up Main Street toward the depot. He picked up his bags, walked across the street to the hotel and checked in. Martin immediately drew a cool bath and opened the windows. Shortly after, he sank into a deep sleep in his first night in Cherokee, Iowa.

Schuster Building, Cherokee, Iowa. Popma's Barber Shop at railing, lower left. *Courtesy of Cherokee Historical Society.*

Al Popma, age 82. 1967 *Courtesy of The Cherokee Times.*

Chapter Eight

Martin awoke bright and early Thursday morning, determined to shave, bathe and be out the door before it got too hot to wear a shirt and tie. He planned to head to the barbershop, then search the local papers--he was surprised to learn Cherokee had two--to find more permanent lodging. The Lewis was impressive and comfortable but his meager savings from the Marshfield shop didn't grant him the luxury of an extended stay.

Al Popma was just opening his shop when Martin came down the steps. A bell above the door rang, and in front of the owner stood a tall, well-dressed young man commencing to sweat just a little.

"You don't appear to need a haircut or a shave mister. What can I do for you?"

"Well, sir, I saw an ad that you were looking for assistants, and I'm here to apply."

Al grinned. "That ad was from five years ago. Did you come here from China?"

"Well, no. Wisconsin, actually. I knew the newspaper wasn't current when I read it, but I thought maybe you could still use another barber."

"Well, to tell the truth, right now we could use another man. I run this shop with my cousin, Walt, and as you can see, we have an open chair. Walt and his father ran the business, and last February his dad passed away. Right now, we're busier than termites in a sawmill. We don't need an apprentice, though; I want a man with experience."

Martin smiled a little. "I've worked at the trade for a while now. I consider myself fairly experienced."

"What's your name, young man?"

"Martin Treptow, sir."

At that, the proprietor's eyes grew wide, and he ran over to vigorously shake Martin's hand. "By God, you're the fella who caught Wilson McDaniel at the train station in Sioux City! It was my brother's shop over in Marcus that he robbed. He took $43.00, and some of his best scissors and razors. Gott in Himmel! If you hadn't tackled him the other day, he might still be running."

"I didn't exactly tackle him, sir, but thank you just the same."

"Treptow, you might be just the man I need around here. When can you start?"

"Right now I'm staying at the Lewis, and if it's okay with you, I'd like to spend the rest of the day looking for lodging. I can start tomorrow if you'd like."

"Tomorrow it is then. I'll expect you to come early and help me set up the shop. Can you be here at seven a.m.?"

"Sir, I'll be here at six."

"If you show up at six you'll be waiting for me. Seven is plenty early, and one other thing…"

"Yes, sir?"

"Don't call me 'sir'. Makes me feel old. I'm 'Al' to everybody in town."

Al turned down Main Street at six forty-five the next morning, figuring he'd get to the shop ready early, and set up the chair for his new hire. He was hoping for another busy morning. Every day of the heatwave convinced Al and Walt that moving the shop to the basement of the Schuster Building was a good idea. It was cooler in the subterranean shop, and the new electric fans Al installed had all the men in town accelerating their haircut schedules. It also seemed like more of the men were splurging on a haircut and shave rather than spending an hour in the taverns. He knew the wives were getting less afraid to tell their husbands to get home to their families. Al figured if prohibition was coming, business might just pick up even more.

The first thing he noticed when he looked down the street was Martin, sitting on the top stair, spit shining his shoes. He stood straight when Al approached, and said "Good morning, sir."

"It's Al. Not 'sir,' just Al. Gott in Himmel, I swear you'll make a fine soldier someday. By the way, I never asked. What do people call you?"

"I'm fine with Martin. But folks call me Trep."

"Trep. Trep." Al repeated the name to himself, test driving the sound. "Yeah, I like that. Strong. Earnest. So, let's get started, Trep. I assume you have your own kit."

"Yes, sir …er, Al, I do."

They walked down the stairs together, and thus began Martin's Cherokee barbering career.

Chapter Nine

Business picked up shortly before noon, after the asylum's early shift. Al had told him all about the state hospital. Before the turn of the century, the Iowa legislature spent three years deciding, first, whether to fund a state hospital for the insane, and then where to place the facility. Ultimately, the lawmakers elected to locate the hospital in northwestern Iowa, and in April 1894, Cherokee was awarded the contract. Work began eight years later in 1902, and the hospital began taking patients as soon as the main buildings were completed. By 1913, the asylum housed over 1,000 patients, and included a large farming operation. The facility's first official title was the "Iowa Lunatic Asylum." As more services were offered, it was not unusual for local residents to know someone who was or had been a patient there. Not coincidently, local folks more frequently began calling the operation simply "the state hospital."

The barbershop stayed busy through the lunch hour and serviced a steady stream of customers until closing time. Al kept an eye on Martin. He didn't talk much, but he responded to comments and asked enough questions to seem interested without being nosey.

In very little time, Al became not only Martin's boss, but also a good friend. Al enjoyed having a good conversationalist in the shop, not only for the customers but in the times when business was slow. And Martin found Al to be an all-around interesting fellow. Al made no secret of his religious convictions, and he conducted himself accordingly. His cussing, for example. "Shit" was uttered solely as a literal descriptive. God might be identified, but never in vain. If the situation called for an expletive of mild surprise, or perhaps admiration, Al would let loose with a "Gott in Himmel!" Once in a while Martin might hear a "Scheisse!" if Al was caught off guard. "Scheisse! Was that a mouse?" Al was very rarely given to complete red faced, clinched fist, bug-eyed anger, but on those very rare occasions, the epithet of choice was "By the holy G!" with every word accented. That was Martin's signal to disappear into the back room and rearrange the tonics.

Al installed electric fans before anyone else, and the shop's magazine pile always included current issues of *Popular Science Monthly*. That made it all the more amusing to Martin when Al would launch into his famous tirade about how the world was moving too fast, and how he missed the good old days. Al once told a traveling salesman that a person hardly ever stepped in horseshit downtown anymore. Martin wasn't sure if he was bragging or complaining. Some customers found it odd to hear these comments from a man barely in his thirties, but of course these were different times. In Al's short life, man had conquered the sky, he'd rendered the buggy obsolete and fantastic inventions of the generation -- telephones, electric lights, movies and phonographs-- were taken for granted. Martin didn't find Al inconsistent at all. The man was optimistic about how technology might benefit the body, yet he worried about its toll on the soul.

Martin hadn't encountered many people who shared his love of history. His teacher back at the country school knew dates and times and places, but eight grades in one room didn't afford her the luxury of discussing details with those who might have more than passing interest. His father told him tales of the old country that his own father remembered. The Ermatingers spun yarns of Indian encounters and the end of the fur trade. Frank Dolezal, the Marshfield raconteur, had a tale of adventure for every day of the week. Martin enjoyed them all, but their stories were personal anecdotes.

Talking to Al was different. His knowledge of people and events surpassed Martin's, and he possessed a unique sense of perspective that sometimes left Martin pondering long after they'd locked up for the night.

One late afternoon they were sweeping up after the last customer of the day, an itinerant leather smith who was passing through town, plying his rapidly vanishing trade.

"Trep, ten years ago that fella had a big shop in Sutherland, and folks would come from all over the county to buy his whips. Now he can't afford to feed his family. The one thing he's good at doesn't count for a plugged nickel any more.

"We live in a unique time, Trep. Civilization has always marched forward, but really, how much did things change from 800 A.D. to 840, or even 1700 to 1740? Now look at the last 40 years. Imagine Thomas Jefferson coming back and being told he could sit in Monticello and talk to someone in New York! How would you like to see the look on Ben Franklin's face when you pulled a cord and turned on an electric light? Gott in Himmel, imagine flying over the Alps with Hannibal in an aeroplane?

"Forty years, Trep, all that in just forty years. Up until now, except maybe inventing the wheel or learning how to build a fire, we've moved forward in stutters and stumbles. Now we're taking giant leaps. Trep, someone who died just 50 years ago wouldn't recognize the world today. I thank the good Lord for letting me be there in these exciting times, but I feel bad for folks like that leather smith who are getting passed by."

"Al, I guess we're lucky to be harvesting something that grows faster than trees."

"Never looked at it that way, exactly, Trep. But I suppose you're right."

Chapter Ten

The shop was busy all the next week. By Saturday, Martin was seeing repeat customers, coming in for a shave, or just lingering in front of one of the electric fans, until Al gave them the eye. In the midafternoon, during a rare lull, and without so much as a "by the way…" Al asked, "Trep, can you swim?"

"Can I swim? Of course, I can swim. Why?"

"Well, I'm taking the family to Okoboji tomorrow. There's a resort there and we can swim and take boat rides. It's a long drive and we'll be leaving early. I thought maybe you'd like to join us.' Then he smiled. "I just don't want my new barber to drown."

"When should I be at your house?"

"Gott in Himmel Trep. If I tell you to be there by 6, you'll be there at 5:30. Come at 6:30, and we'll leave at 6."

It was already 85 degrees and humid when they got to the lake. Donnie, the Popma's four year old son, couldn't wait to get in the water. Al's wife, Louise watched the boy, and Martin and Al rented lockers and changed into their swimming trunks. Once they got in the lake, Al joined his family, and in the middle of a hundred other swimmers, Martin was alone with his thoughts. He floated on his back, enjoying the cool water and warm sun. He thought of summer days on the farm, getting in the Chippewa when the chores were done, and swimming in the Mill Pond after they moved to Bloomer.

He thought about the great swim race back in Rice Lake, between Gus and the boy from Cameron. His mother had written him about the new hydroelectric dam near Chippewa Falls that would swallow farms and create a vast lake on the river, and he wondered if anyone from the railroad crew was working on the project. His aquatic reverie was broken up by Al's yell.

"Trep, let's get some lunch!"

"Tell you what, Al, I'll buy. You drove, and I'm sure you're about to give me a great big raise on Monday."

"What?"

They'd only known each other a week so Al had to look at Martin for a moment to be sure he was kidding.

The soda fountain was just off the beach. It offered a good view of the water and everyone who walked by. Martin was finishing his lunch when he noticed a group of laughing young women approaching. As they passed in front of him, one sang a line from *Daisy Bell*… *"I'm half crazy, all for the love of you."* Martin could tell she was teasing one of her friends; at least it seemed that way. But he recognized the voice-- the same one he'd heard at the American Theatre. He stared for a moment and noticed that beautiful voice was emanating from the prettiest girl. And just as he looked away, he thought-he wasn't sure-but maybe just for a second- that she'd looked right at him.

Chapter Eleven

The heat wave broke early the following week, and Al planned to spend the weekend working around the house. Martin was left to his own devices, and Friday evening he planned to see *"The Secret of the Submarine,"* playing at the American. Europe was much on everyone's mind, and it was no coincidence that the first installment of the *Submarine* serial was released only weeks after the *Lusitania* was torpedoed.

Fridays were busy days at the barber shop, and August 11th was no exception. Martin stayed late to clean up, and by the time he got to the theatre, the only seats left were in the front row. No sooner had he sat down when he noticed the piano player. It was the same young woman he'd seen a week ago at Okoboji. The movie hadn't started, and she was arranging her sheets. As Martin sat down, she looked up, and for just a moment, Martin was sure their eyes met. Martin thought she'd looked his way several times during the movie, and of course he wouldn't have noticed had he'd not been looking at her as well. He considered introducing himself when the movie ended, but as the lights went up, a friend of Al's recognized him and said "Trep, how ya doin'? Let's go get a beer." When he turned around the young lady was gone.

Martin was taking to Cherokee, and he realized early on that his arrival couldn't have been better timed. Thanks to the heat wave-- and Al's fan-cooled basement barbershop—Martin made dozens of acquaintances in the first weeks. The dry weather also allowed folks to drive out of town on weekends. The late summer roads were rarely muddy or rutted, so on Sundays Al and Martin would head out in Al's Model T and drive around the county.

One afternoon after they'd changed a tire a few miles east of the city, Al suggested they enjoy a cigar before heading back into town. They'd stopped on Highway 5, where the road turned south to Aurelia. 1916 would produce record crops in western Iowa, and despite the Sabbath, farmers were out harvesting the last of the oats. The two men needed only to look to the means of production to know which farms were the most prosperous; some utilized the latest gas-powered machinery, others still maintained a team of horses.

"Cherokee County is a resting giant, Trep. See these fields? That's some of the best farmland in Iowa. That's his brawn, his sinew. The city is his heart, and his artery is the railroad."

"Anthropomorphism."

"Anthro what?"

"Anthropomorphism. Giving human traits to an animal, or an object. People have always done that."

"Gott in Himmel, Trep! Where'd you learn a word like that?"

"I read, Al. We talk about Mother Nature and Father Time, don't we? I'll tell you a story. When I was a kid, my dad took me and my little sister with him to Chippewa Falls to buy a new wagon. When we left, my father told my sister the old wagon was sad, saying "Wait, don't leave me behind!". She cried halfway home, and she still gets mad at him whenever he teases her about it."

Al looked down the road to the west. "I think we're gonna see a new artery, though. More and more cars. They'll pave these roads, and then what happens to the trains? You know, Trep, the first artery was the river. The Indians used it, and they say the James Gang would hide out along the banks."

"I should've asked."

"What?"

"Nothing. I think you're right, Al. In twenty years, folks will all be driving to town. Maybe in a hundred years they'll have flying cars. One thing's for sure, Cherokee won't be just a railroad town anymore."

Martin realized too late that he'd hit a nerve. "Trep, I was in Sioux City awhile back, and I heard two traveling salesmen talking about Cherokee. One said, 'It's just a railroad town,' and he turned up his nose. I'd liked to have punched that guy.

"Have you met anyone yet who wasn't friendly? Anyone who didn't work hard or provide for his family? The women are good mothers, and pretty soon now they'll be smart voters, but don't tell Louise I said that. These are good, God-fearing folks, Trep. Count the churches next time you walk through town. I'll bet you every farmer who's out harvesting today had to clear his conscience to spend Sunday in the field.

"Railroad town! Scheisse!"

As they drove back to town, Al told Martin about "Old Cherokee," the original settlement north of town, and how speculators had gambled on where the railroad depot would be built. When they learned it was going in a mile or so to the south, folks simply up and moved their houses and businesses to the

"New Cherokee," and the original townsite was forgotten. That part of the story surprised him. In the short time he'd lived there, Martin came to appreciate how much the people held on to their past. Folks knew when their grandparents arrived and where they came from. Sometimes they still spoke their language. On the other hand, people couldn't wait to tell out-of-towners how modern and progressive the city was. When Al's resting giant stood up, he had one foot stepping forward, and the other holding traction in the past. Martin thought that compromise fit the town pretty well.

Chapter Twelve

On Wednesday afternoon, August 23rd, Al suggested they close early. It was between pay periods at the hospital and business was slow, and the weather just happened to be late August Iowa perfect. Al gave Martin a choice: they could catch a base ball game at Nohanis Park or they could go to the Happy Hour and see "*The Raiders*." Martin looked out at the cloudless blue sky, and a half hour later, both men were sitting behind third base with a beer and a cigar. The game was close, and Al was good company, but Martin's mind kept wandering downtown, to that pretty piano player at the American.

The next morning, Al's wife stopped by the shop. When the boys headed to the ball game the previous afternoon, Louise and some friends took in the movie.

"Did you enjoy it?" Martin asked.

"We certainly did. But I didn't know who to root for. It was about a scheme to ruin a railroad, and I wasn't sure if I wanted the rich fellow to win in the end."

Louise had long favored both prohibition and the suffrage, and Al had remarked more than once that she was "getting a little too progressive." Martin knew her comments about "the rich fellow" were intended just to get a rise out of her husband.

"And do you know what else? Ms. Van de Steeg, the piano player at the American, is now at the Happy Hour as well. She even sang a song at the end. She's so pretty, and she has such a beautiful voice."

"Van de Steeg? What's her first name?" Martin asked.

"Why Mr. Treptow, why do you ask?" Mrs. Popma teased.

"Well…um. I just thought…uh… if I happen to meet her on the street it would be polite to know her first name."

"Martin Treptow, I don't believe you for a moment. But just so you can be polite, her name is Pearl."

Martin uttered a very quiet "Hmm." The Popmas made no attempt to hide their smiles.

The next few weeks granted Martin no opportunity to meet Pearl on the street, but he was otherwise learning quickly that Al's comments about friendly people were not merely small town chamber of commerce hyperbole. Every other day featured a social gathering of some sort in Cherokee or one of the neighboring towns. On Monday, September 11th, Al suggested they drive to Aurelia on Thursday afternoon for the Farmers and Merchants Picnic. "It's only seven miles. The weather is supposed to be nice, and there'll be a dance after. And Trep, I'll tell you what. We'll open at nine on Friday."

Al's weather forecast was accurate, as usual. By mid afternoon, the temperature rose to the mid 70's, and Tuesday's rains erased any lingering humidity. Cherokee County folks needed only to look at the turning sumac to know to take full advantage of the autumn reprieve. By the late afternoon, when Al and Martin arrived in Aurelia, the children's games were in full swing and the beer garden was near capacity. Just after six, as the last attendee was finishing supper, Aurelia's mayor stepped to the children's award stand and asked everyone's attention.

"As you all know, we'll be moving inside at seven for the big dance. To get you ready for the music, we have a special treat this evening. She's going to sing a selection of Christian and patriotic songs, and if you young folks promise to behave, perhaps some popular songs as well. Please give a big Aurelia welcome to Cherokee's wonderful young vocalist, Miss Pearl Van de Steeg!"

Martin looked at Al, and before he could say anything, Al smiled at him and said "Yeah, I heard. Would you like to get closer to the stage?"

Pearl acknowledged the introduction just as Martin and Al settled in near the near the front. For a second, Martin thought she'd made eye contact, but the moment passed quickly, and he couldn't be sure. Pearl began with *"Nearer my God to Thee"* followed by another religious selection. She then took a short break, and in Martin's opinion, gamely endured some inappropriate flirtation from the mayor. She returned to the stage for the patriotic set, singing *"Old Glory"* and *"America I Love You."* She then spoke to the picnic goers.

"Next I'd like to honor all the young soldiers fighting right now in France. We're so fortunate to have all our loved ones here at home." She then broke into a rousing rendition of *"It's a Long Way to Tipperary,"* accompanied by the rhythmic clapping of her audience.

It was getting close to seven, and after she caught her breath, Pearl smiled and asked the teenagers, "Would you like to hear a popular song?" Eliciting the expected response, she launched into an enthusiastic rendition of *"Alexander's Ragtime Band."*

"Come on and hear, come on and hear

Alexander's Ragtime Band

Come on and hear, come on and hear

It's the best band in the land..."

She began the next stanza, and even the old women seemed to enjoy the popular song. Halfway through the chorus, however, a funny thing happened. Just after she sang *"That's the bestest band what am..."* her staccato soprano slowed to a sensuous contralto, and she almost whispered, *"Honey Lamb, come on along, come on along, let me take you by the hand."* And she was looking directly at Martin.

No sooner had she sung *"by the hand,"* when Pearl returned to her faster, higher key, and finished the song. It happened so quickly the old women had no time to be righteously indignant. When the song ended, they weren't entirely sure what they'd heard. The men not so much heard it as felt it--for most of the young men, their first time; for many of the old men, their first time in a long time. The moment wasn't lost on Martin and Al. They looked at each other wide eyed, and Al summed up the moment.

"Gott in Himmel."

A large tent was set up in the park for the dance, and the crowd moved inside. Some families made their way to their cars or walked to the train station. Martin and Al headed to the beer garden. When he got to the bar, Martin was pleasantly surprised to find himself standing next to Pearl.

"You have a beautiful voice."

"Why, thank you," she responded. She looked at him but said nothing further.

Martin wasn't quite sure what to say next. "I've noticed you before..." he began.

"Should I alert the police?"

"Well, I mean I've seen you play at the theatre, and I've heard you sing. I sort of thought you had seen me before too. I thought just now you were watching me as you sang."

"Well, aren't we Mr. Confidence? First of all, I have no idea what you're talking about, and secondly, if you believe we made some 'connection' it's simply because I personalize my songs for my audience."

"I'm sorry, I didn't mean..."

"Did you like it?" and now she smiled, just a little.

"Yes, I did. I think every man at the picnic did."

"I hope I didn't give some of the old women a heart attack." This time she smiled with her eyes as well.

"Do you have a name?" she asked.

"My name is Martin. Martin Treptow. But people call me Trep."

"Trep? Do you like 'Trep'?"

"Yes, I think it's...strong, earnest."

"Earnest? It's a dog's name. 'Come here, Trep.' 'That's a good boy, Trep.' Martin is a fine name. When we meet again, you'll be Martin, not Trep."

"When we meet again? So, I may call on you?"

"May you call on me? How wonderfully quaint. Yes, you may. Now, Martin, do you have a cigarette?"

"I do." Martin deftly pulled the small metal box from his pocket, removed one cigarette, and offered to light it for her.

"You're not surprised a woman would ask for a cigarette?"

"It's 1916. A woman can have a cigarette if she wants."

"How very modern of you, Mr. Treptow. But I must come clean. I don't really smoke. It would raise absolute havoc with my voice. I simply wanted to see how you would react."

"Well, Miss Van de Steeg, I hope I passed the audition. And now I shall come clean as well. I was hoping to meet you today. Do you now think less of me?

"To the contrary, I'm quite flattered. Now in 1916, Martin, may a woman ask a gentleman to dance?"

"She may, and this gentleman would accept."

Pearl was surprised Martin didn't fumble and stutter when she asked for a cigarette. She also was pleasantly surprised that a man from the northern Wisconsin woods could be so light on his feet.

Chapter Thirteen

5 weeks earlier - Thursday, August 3rd, 1916.

The old Empress Theatre was now the Happy Hour. The new owners, wanting to provide folks a familiar talent, reached out to the piano player at the American, to see if she might play their theatre as well. And so, on Thursday afternoon Ms. Pearl Van de Steeg was on her way to meet the new proprietors.

As she passed by Popma's Barber Shop, she noticed a muscular young man having a cigarette on the top stair. She'd not seen him before and made note of his confident carriage. That night, following her first performance at the Happy Hour, she saw Louise Popma and casually asked if her husband had hired a new man.

"Oh yes, Martin Treptow. He's from northern Wisconsin. He seems like a nice young man. Now, Pearl, why do you ask?"

"Just curious," Pearl responded, but did a poor job of hiding her smile.

"I think he's going to Okoboji with us on Saturday. Maybe the two of you can meet."

"I am in no hurry to meet him, or anyone else," she quickly replied. "But it might be a good day for a swim."

Pearl talked some friends into joining her at the lake, suggesting a day at the resort would be a pleasant way to spend a warm Saturday. They arrived early and were in the water before most of the crowd got there. By the time the Popmas arrived, Pearl and her friends were out of the water and everyone's hair was back in place. Pearl's friends thought she was taking longer than usual with her makeup, but Pearl always made sure her look was just right. Lemon juice for the bleached skin, then powder, then a little rouge, then powder again. Pearl never liked the papier poudre, but it fit easily into a purse. Finally, the lips. Accentuated, but never painted.

Just after noon, as they walked along the shore, Pearl spotted the family outside the soda fountain. She saw Martin immediately, and as the young women passed in front of them, she sang a single line from *Daisy Bell*. She flashed a quick look at Martin and looked away the moment their eyes met.

All in all, she was quite pleased with the encounter.

The following Friday, she was back at the American, playing the background piano for *"The Secret of the Submarine."* The theatre was crowded, and just before the film started, she was surprised to see Martin taking a seat in the first row. The current installment was new to theatres and Pearl was not familiar with the music, so she had little opportunity to look away from her sheets. Nevertheless, she managed to steal a glance at Martin from time to time and was happy to see he appeared to notice her as well.

She worked almost every evening in late August, and when school started in early September, she helped teach physical education to the high school girls. As a result, unless Martin happened into one of the theatres, she had no opportunity to see him. It wasn't until the Farmers and Merchants Picnic that she saw him again, and when she stepped on the stage, she resolved to get his attention. The sultry octave drop was something she'd heard other singers perform but had little chance to try it herself during her religious and patriotic arias in Cherokee. She hesitated for just a moment, lifted her head, and focused her gaze on Martin: "*Honey Lamb, come on along, come on along, Let me take you by the hand…*"

Chapter Fourteen

It was already Friday morning in northern France when the Aurelia festivities ended. At that moment, divisions of British and Canadian troops went over the top to assault German trenches during the Battle of the Somme. By the end of the day, British casualties alone would number almost 30,000, and all told, over 100,000 young men would never have a first dance with a lovely young lady.

Chapter Fifteen

Martin indeed called on Pearl, and their first date lead to a second, and a third. Somehow Martin and Pearl found time in their busy lives to spend time together, and soon casual interest begat mutual infatuation. Martin always felt like he was just a step behind Pearl, but her smile and those dark eyes kept him scrambling to keep up. She was worldly--not in a way that generated talk--but she'd been to Chicago and unlike most of the Cherokee women her age, her hopes and dreams didn't end at the county line. It made Martin's day to make her laugh, and when they'd meet after a performance and she'd touch his hand, he couldn't help but to draw a quick breath and crack a broad smile. Later, alone in his room back at Mrs. Swenson's, Martin would play out the scene in his mind, and swear he'd never again grin like an idiot when their hands touched. But the next time it happened he'd do it all over again.

Pearl had noticed Martin's manner the first time she saw him outside the barber shop. Just a subtle arch of the neck transforms confidence into conceit, but Pearl saw nothing but gentle strength in his carriage. He was versed in the events of the day and had the rare ability to talk religion and politics with a civil level of discourse. He was witty, and he made her laugh. Martin also made Pearl feel like she was no longer alone. As long as she could remember, people told her what a marvelous voice she had. Her piano teachers always said she was their most talented pupil. All the compliments were a little embarrassing, and there was really no one to talk to about it. She was sure her friends would just think she was bragging. But she could tell everything to Martin. Still, Pearl prided herself on her independence, and she was not entirely comfortable with this new vulnerability. Alone at night she'd tell herself she'd be more careful about allowing him a direct conduit to her heart. But the next time their hands touched she'd open herself up all over again.

Fortunately, perhaps, their lives left little time for negative reflection. The Empress and the Happy Hour featured new movies every week, and in between, Pearl was constantly asked to sing at some pageant or church service. Down the steps at Popma's, Martin was barbering at a pace far beyond anything he'd seen back in Marshfield. A man could take the train from the great cities of the east-Pittsburgh, Cleveland, even New York, and ride straight through to California. And if he took the Burlington Northern out of Chicago, he'd pass right through Cherokee. Now and then folks would decide that Cherokee, Iowa was a good a place as any to end the journey for the day. Others would come intending to stop in town. By 1916, the state hospital was one of the largest of its kind in the Midwest, and expansion meant a steady stream of contractors and salesmen. If they had business up the hill, and someone they wanted to impress, they'd stop in for a shave and a haircut.

It was late in the day on October 30, 2016. Martin and Al were reading the *Cherokee Times* and discussing the various electors for the November 7th presidential election. Cherokee hadn't seen the sun for a week, and a brisk wind had blown off the last of the fall color. More than one old timer had come into the shop telling Martin and Al, "There's snow in them clouds." Martin would learn in the coming months that business dropped off significantly during the winter, as rail traffic slowed, and the farmers stayed home.

Al was ready to close when a well-dressed man stepped through the door. His luggage indicated he was in town on business, or perhaps stopping for the night before traveling to Sioux City or Des Moines. "Shave and a haircut?" Martin asked.

"I think I'm due."

The men started discussing the events of the day immediately after Martin's straight razor left the man's throat. "I see you have a sample ballot there. So tell me, is this a Wilson Town or a Hughes town?"

"Truth be told", Al responded, "I think Roosevelt and the progressives will win the vote here."

"Progressive, eh? I suppose change is good."

Martin was sure Al would lunge at that opportunity, and sure enough, he swallowed the bait to the gills.

"Change? What more change do we need? Everyone has to have indoor plumbing now. You tell me if your parents would've been comfortable having a water closet right next to where they cooked their food. A good horse isn't good enough; everyone needs an automobile. And now even the kids want to drive. And there are no more quiet evenings with the lamps. Now it's electric lights, and it's daylight all the time. And do we men have a say in these matters? I'll tell you it's less and less. Last summer Iowa defeated suffrage only by 2,000 votes. Before you know it, the women will be voting, and they'll be running this town. And you know what they'll be voting for, don't you? Prohibition! You better enjoy your beers now, because before you know it, we'll be dry."

Martin knew Al was just getting started.

"And the kids today... all this new machinery, these kids don't have to work. Maybe one out of ten can still groom a horse.

When they don't work, they get lazy and they don't respect authority. But still they want. 'Buy me this, father, buy me that!' "Gott in Himmel, last month my niece told her father, 'We need a Victrola, no one has a gramophone anymore.' And what does she listen to? Ragtime! Blues! That isn't music! You can't make out half the words, and the ones you hear out don't mean anything. Give me Enrico Caruso. Now that's music."

The man in the barber chair smiled very slightly through Al's tirade; not enough of a smile to mock, just enough to let Martin know that he had a little broader view of the world.

"You know, very soon you might have a machine in your home that will play music for you without the need for a Victrola."

In an instant the luddite vanished, and the man met the subscriber to *Popular Mechanics*. "What kind of a machine?"

"Have you ever heard of Professor Culver, from Beloit College? He's a physics teacher there, and he's using wireless telegraphy to send signals of the current time to the local high schools."

"You mean wireless code? Like what the radio man on the *Titanic* sent to the *Carpathia*?" Al asked.

"Better than that. My company has developed something called a vacuum tube, and by manipulating the sound waves-we call it amplitude modulation-voices can be transmitted, and even music."

"What's your company?" Martin asked.

"I work for Westinghouse Electric. Tomorrow morning I'm meeting with the managers of the state hospital. They're interested in a new steam turbine generator."

"Tell me more about this transmitter."

"Well, sir, it's been proven that radio waves travel farther than anyone imagined. If we can build a strong enough transmitter, and a large enough antenna, Professor Culver could play your Caruso in Beloit and you could listen to it at home here in Cherokee. And eventually, there might be stations in Chicago, and even Sioux City and Des Moines, and you'll have your choice of music."

"What if I want to hear something they're not playing?" Al asked.

"Well, I suppose you could dial up Professor Culver on the telephone and make a request."

Al put his scissors down and stared out at the basement steps.

"Gott in Himmel. Imagine that."

Chapter Sixteen

Cherokee County, in fact, voted progressive in the November election. The state, however, gave its electoral votes to Charles Evans Hughes, the Republican candidate. Iowa's electoral votes gave Hughes a total of 254, twenty-three behind Woodrow Wilson, the incumbent. Wilson's campaign motto: "He kept us out of war."

In Europe, Britain and France abandoned the Somme offensive, having gained less than five miles in five months. The opposing armies suffered over a million dead and wounded, one of whom was a short Austrian corporal named Adolf Hitler. A month later, the Battle of Verdun concluded. Over 10 months, the combatants suffered another million casualties.

Back in Cherokee, folks enjoyed a brief respite from war news as winter approached. The great armies stood down temporarily, and in mid-December, President Wilson asked the warring nations to offer peace terms. Martin was beginning to consider his own peace terms, if he couldn't find the perfect Christmas gift for Pearl. By Saturday, December 22nd, he'd still not selected the ideal present. The *Times* that morning published a list of last-minute gifts for him and her, but he was uncomfortable buying perfume or toiletries, and a Kodak was hardly romantic. He finally settled on a small vanity box. Inside, he placed a note saying, "The bearer is entitled to two Columbia Grafonola records of her choice, the tariff being one kiss per record."

Martin had recently taken a fancy to fine cigars. Pearl forbade him from smoking when they were together indoors, but she liked it when he held the cigar between his teeth and smiled. It displayed confidence, and - though she'd never admit it to anyone – virility. She'd decided on his gift a month earlier: a box of El Phantos, encased in a polished wood cigar box.

Martin enjoyed holiday dinner with the Popmas, and Pearl spent the day with family. In the evening they met at the opera house, and enjoyed a vaudeville show, "The Girl and the Tramp." They exchanged their gifts afterwards, and Pearl happily accepted the tariff.

The start of the new year found them both busy. Early January was mild, and the barbershop enjoyed more business than they anticipated. Pearl was working seven nights a week, accompanying the new 1917 movies. Then, beginning Sunday, January 21st, a two-day blizzard buried the state under two feet of snow. The temperature plunged for two weeks, rising only in time for another blizzard on February 4th. The old folks compared the storms to "The Great Blizzard of '88", a weather event that had become a Midwest legend. In fact, Pearl's sheet music included a copy of *Nebraska's Fearless Maid,* a song about schoolteacher Minnie Freeman, who braved the storm and saved her young students.

World events also had folks talking. On January 19th, British Intelligence intercepted an encoded telegram sent by Alfred Zimmerman, the German States' Secretary for Foreign Affairs, to their embassies in Washington and Mexico City. Zimmerman proposed an alliance between Mexico and Germany and promised to help Mexico regain territories lost to the United States over the previous 75 years. On February 3rd, a German submarine sank the *Housatonic*, an American merchant ship. Later that day, Wilson spoke to Congress and severed diplomatic relations with Germany.

Chapter Seventeen

Johnny, get your gun, get your gun, get your gun,

Johnny, show the Hun you're a son-of-a-gun,

Hoist the flag and let her fly,

Yankee Doodle do or die.

Over There, George M. Cohen 1917

The American public learned of the Zimmerman Telegram in March, and on April 6, 1917, Congress voted to declare war. Six senators, one each from the nearby states of North Dakota, Wisconsin, and Nebraska opposed the war, and three of Iowa's representatives voted nay as well.

The erstwhile peace candidate moved swiftly after that to place the nation on a war footing and win the hearts and the minds of its citizens. In early 1917, George Creel, a Colorado journalist who supported Wilson sent the newly re-elected President a long letter outlining a program to encourage Americans to support joining the war. Wilson was impressed; Creel proposed a nationwide propaganda blitz, encouraging patriotism and focusing on American values. Only a week after the formal declaration of war, Wilson created the Committee on Public Information, and appointed Creel to oversee the department.

Perhaps better than anyone else at the time, Creel understood the persuasive power of early 20th century media. He knew almost every village had a movie theatre. CPI money produced numerous patriotic films, and some of Hollywood's biggest stars – Mary Pickford, Charlie Chaplin, Al Jolson – were enlisted through CPI to sell Liberty Bonds. Creel also knew that more and more American families were buying Victrolas, and he encouraged songwriters and musicians to pen and perform songs to inspire patriotic ardor. Georg M. Cohen's *Over There* was followed by hundreds of nationalistic ditties. CPI also flooded the nation with patriotic posters, many drawn by famous artists and illustrators, to get all Americans on board.

Creel also recognized, however, the degree to which ordinary Americans valued the opinions of their neighbors. He knew that wherever Americans gathered - movie theatres, schools, churches, lodge meetings - the war was much on people's minds. Creel's CPI hired thousands of "Four-Minute Men" to give short patriotic speeches around the nation at theaters, plays, picnics, and other public gatherings.

No age group and no segment of the American population escaped Creel's attention. There was a "War Savings Pledge" to encourage citizens to buy war bonds, a "Housewife's Pledge" to encourage families not to waste food and ultimately to support rationing. There were pledges for farmers, for factory workers, and even for children. Keeping with the spirit of the times, there also was a "Temperance Pledge" intended to steel the resolve of America's new fighting men.

Immediately after the declaration of war, President Wilson called for volunteers to serve. National Guard units around the nation were directed to open recruiting stations to fill the ranks. The Third Iowa Infantry had spent the last ten months on the Mexican border, and only returned home in February. Recruiting got underway immediately with the goal of swelling the ranks of every company, including Cherokee's Company M, to 100 men.

Unfortunately, by mid-May, the nation as a whole counted only 73,000 volunteers, and on May 18th, Congress passed the Selective Service Act. Class One-the most likely draftees-consisted of unmarried men with no dependents, physically fit, between the ages of 21 and 30. Unlike the Civil War draft, no substitutes were allowed. In August, the Class One age range was expanded to 18 to 45. By the end of the war, almost 3 million men had been drafted into service.

Shortly after the National Guard units were federalized, Major Douglas MacArthur suggested that a division be formed from the various state units that "would stretch over the whole country like a rainbow." The new 42nd Division ultimately included units from 26 states and the District of Columbia. When the 93rd Infantry, comprised mostly of Negro soldiers from New York and New England petitioned to join the Rainbow Division, Major MacArthur was reputed to have responded, "There is no color black in the rainbow." Colonel William Haywood one of the 93rd's commanders, was rumored to have replied, "There also is no white in a rainbow."

Chapter Eighteen

When war was declared, Wilson hoped the existing National Guard units and volunteers would be enough to man what would become the American Expeditionary Force. However, anyone who had followed the course of the war over the past three years knew the American effort would have to be considerably more cannon-fodder-intensive.

Draft eligible men throughout the nation faced difficult decisions. In western Iowa and other parts of the upper Midwest, the issue was complicated by the German heritage of many of its residents. On March 19th, the *Semi-Weekly Democrat* ran an article about a Cleghorn farmer who was flying the flag of Imperial Germany, and who, according to witnesses, "made the remark that if war came, he would do all in his power to help the German government." On April 16th, Michael Schuh, a blacksmith from Royal, just north of Cherokee, was arrested and fined $25.00 for cutting down a flagpole and making "unpatriotic remarks." Back in northwest Wisconsin, pastors of the Chippewa County churches voted only after much deliberation to no longer conduct any services in German.

Since the American Revolution, there had been no intervals of peace lasting long enough to shield an entire generation from combat. America's Pax Romana lasted only 33 years, from 1865 to 1898, and even then, a father could die at Petersburg, and his son could be killed charging up San Juan Hill. Early on, the Treptow men were lucky. Grandpa Martin was too young for the German wars of unification, and he emigrated before the Franco-Prussian War. Albert was too old for the Spanish American War.

The winning streak ended with his son, however. When America entered the war in the spring of 1917, Martin was all of 23.

Chapter Nineteen

Spring had finally arrived in Cherokee, but neither Martin nor Pearl could find the opportunity to enjoy it. As the roads dried and the temperature rose, Cherokee saw more visitors—businessmen, visiting family members, and tourists, and it seemed like every male who showed up in town sported two day's growth or hair that needed cutting—or both. Pearl was fully occupied as well. Her employers at the American Theater enjoyed favored status with Paramount, and sometimes received first run films even before Sioux City or Des Moines. When she was not playing at one of the theatres, she was singing somewhere.

The weekend of April 7th brought the nicest weather of the spring. Many of the local farmers gambled and planted their potatoes early the following week. Martin had a rare Saturday free, but Pearl, as usual, did not. On Sunday evening, they vowed to spend the following Sunday together. Pearl suggested that after morning services, she'd drive them to Storm Lake, an hour to the southeast. They planned a picnic and hoped the pleasant weather would hold.

Unfortunately, by mid-week, winter reappeared. Those farmers who had already planted found their efforts frozen in the fields. The weather warmed a little each day, though, and by Sunday morning, the picnic plans were back on. Pearl still brought extra blankets, just in case.

They left church together and walked separately home to change clothes. Martin was waiting on the step an hour later when Pearl drove up. No sooner had he jumped in the front seat when he reached back to peek in the picnic basket, which earned him an immediate slap on the hand. "Get out of there! You'll see what I brought when we get to the lake."

Pearl was smiling, but Martin knew her well enough by that time to comply with her wishes. He did notice, however, that the basket contained four beers.

"You know, Pearl, they're giving you the suffrage hoping you women will vote dry. I don't think a young lady with four beers in her picnic basket is what the legislature has in mind."

"First of all, no one's 'giving us the suffrage.' Women have been fighting for the vote for four decades, and men are finally waking up. Second, Mr. Treptow, this young lady enjoys a beer now and then, thank you. I'm quite aware that we approved the amendment last week. Best we enjoy it while we can."

Pearl handled the car with complete confidence. Martin didn't know any other single woman in Cherokee, or in the entire county for that matter, who owned her own car. He knew some folks in town didn't think it exactly proper that a woman should be driving a car, much less a young, unmarried one who owned her own. Martin also had to endure some ribbing from Al and the regulars at the barber shop about having a woman chauffeur.

Martin didn't mind, however, and he knew Pearl wasn't bothered by a little gossip. She loved the car. From the first day she saw one of the new Dodge Brothers' roadsters at DeJarnett's Auto on West Main Street she knew she wanted one. She made a great deal with the owner, the moment he realized the attractive local celebrity would be the perfect advertisement for the car. It was more expensive than a Model T, but Pearl liked the wire wheels and sleeker styling. It wasn't the car everybody else had.

Martin said little as they drove to the lake, passing through Aurelia, then Alta. The road was still winter-worn, and the open roadster was noisy. Still, Pearl noticed that even when they slowed through the towns, Martin made little attempt at conversation. Finally, they arrived in Storm Lake, and drove through town to the lake. It was a popular picnic area, and by the time they arrived in the early afternoon, families had claimed most of the prime spots. Fortunately, they found a suitable place near the lake, and spread a blanket under a large tree that had just begun teasing out its first spring buds.

"Martin, you didn't say hardly anything on the drive. Are you okay?"

"I'm fine, Pearl. It's the war. It's just… it's a lot to think about."

"Think out loud. We'll think together."

"Well, I've been reading about the war and we've both been watching the newsreels. I don't think this will be like fighting Spain or chasing Pancho Villa. This is going to be like the War Between the States. It's going to be bad, and Americans are going to be dying just like the English and French and Germans and the Russians.

"Al is right. All these new inventions. Our wonderful modern times. Tanks and poison gas and machine guns that shoot a hundred times a second. I remember how aeroplanes were going to bring the world together. Now they use 'em to drop bombs on people."

Pearl looked over at Martin. She expected he'd be downcast, but instead, he met her gaze directly, and he showed her a look she'd never seen before.

83

"But you know what? I can't explain this, Pearl, but in some way, thinking about that danger makes me want to be part of it. I've only told one other person this, but I've never really ever been afraid. I've never had to save myself or save anyone else. Part of me wonders what I'd do. Would I run? Would I be a hero? I guess I'd like to know.

"There's something else, too. Pearl, I've bounced around an awful lot. I didn't think Bloomer or the farm was right for me, and I didn't last but a few months in Marshfield. Since I was old enough to ride the train by myself, I thought, well if one place doesn't fit, I'll just move on. Cherokee is different, Pearl. I liked Al from the very beginning. I could work with him for a long time. And boy, everyone is so friendly. Bloomer folks are friendly, too, but I was never a stranger there. A person gets a real good feeling when strangers accept you right off the bat.

"And there's also…"

"Also what?" Pearl asked.

"Well, you. There's also you. We haven't known each other that long, but I-I've never met anyone like you. What happens to us if I go off to war? I don't mean what if I get killed. I mean what if…will I be the same person when I come back? Will you be the same person? I know it sounds silly, but if I join up, I'd want you to come with me."

Pearl smiled. "Do they have pianos in the trenches?"

"I know you couldn't really join me, but I do think about-I hope-that we have some future, and you said we'd think together. I hope you think that, too."

Pearl was rarely caught by surprise. She sensed opportunity, she weighed the risks, and she acted. Even as Martin became central to her world, she'd considered the war only in abstract terms. So, for a second she was taken aback; the careful planner had never considered that Martin might actually enlist and ship off to France. A weaker individual might have been betrayed by a tear, but Pearl escaped the moment with just a sudden deep breath.

"Martin, I very much want to have a future with you. If you go, I'll support your decision, and I'll pray for you and I'll write you every day and when you get back, the only difference you'll see is that I'll love you even more."

As often as they'd been together since the fall, this was the first time they'd discussed a future together. Pearl thought it best for both of them to lighten the moment.

"And maybe I'll sneak on that troop ship."

Martin kissed her cheek and smiled. "And I won't tell."

"There's something else, Pearl. Am I a traitor for wondering if we should even go to war? President Wilson said just last fall he'd keep us out of the war. And now look at where we are. A man was in the barber shop last week talking about what Eugene Debs said. He said we're going to war because the rich industrialists back east have too much at stake."

"Debs is a socialist! He doesn't know what he's talking about. Martin, the Germans have no respect for America. I don't for one minute believe they would've helped Mexico start a war, but wasn't it still an insult to America to even suggest it? And the submarine warfare… Martin, they're already at war with us. If we're not at war with them, we're naïve and foolish."

"But Germany? I never thought we'd be fighting Germany, Pearl. My grandparents spoke German. My mother and father speak German when they tease each other and pray in German when they're in church. What did you sing in church last Christmas? I sang *Stille Nacht*, and I'll bet you did, too."

"Martin, are you a German, or are you an American? And don't tell me you're a 'German-American'. That means nothing."

"Pearl, this is my country. I'll defend my country, but I'd just feel more comfortable if we were fighting Egypt or Siam. And where do I join—if I join? Do I volunteer for the Third Iowa, or do I go back to Wisconsin?"

Pearl looked at him for a full five seconds. "Where's home, Martin?"

Now it was Martin's turn to pause. "Pearl, I've been thinking about that before all this war stuff—ever since I met you. I can't explain it very well. I miss my family—my mother especially. I miss the farm, and I feel like I never had a real chance to enjoy our new home in town. Someday I want you to come with me to see the farm and Bloomer and meet my family."

"Martin, driving a car is one thing. But a single woman accompanying a single man on a long trip to a small town? I have to think my appearance in town might not be well received. Can one sprain a tongue? We'd certainly find out. Every tongue in Bloomer would be wagging nonstop."

"I'll tell you what. Just before we get off the train in Bloomer, we'll put a pretty white bow in your hair."

Pearl couldn't contain her laughter. "Should I also wear a little button that says 'virgin', or will the white bow be enough?"

Martin had no clever response to that and opted for a smile and a kiss. They sipped their beer and watched the nearby children. After a time, Pearl again prompted Martin to explain himself.

"Sometimes when I feel that I can't explain something the way I'd like to, I use a metaphor. Give me a metaphor, Martin."

"Gosh woman, now you've made it even more difficult. A metaphor? Okay, let me think."

He paused, then began, "I loved—I love Wisconsin. But I needed to breathe. I feel like I can really breathe here. Cherokee is my bellows."

Pearl smiled and shook her head. "That's a terrible metaphor, Martin. Try again. See the buds on that green ash? By summertime those branches will be thick with dark green leaves, and every year those branches grow farther away from the tree. If those branches stop expanding, what happens?"

"The tree won't thrive."

"Exactly, you're branching out Martin, as everyone must if they want to thrive. Now look at the roots."

"I can't see the roots."

"No, you can't. But they're still there. And you can't forget about them. If they're not nurtured, if they're forgotten, the tree dies. You know where your roots are, Martin, and even though you rarely see them, I don't believe that you'll ever forget about those roots."

"Okay, that's a better metaphor. But it's not perfect."

"And why not?"

"I don't plan to drop my clothes in the fall."

"Martin Treptow, on behalf of every citizen of Cherokee County, I thank you for that promise."

They spent the next several hours in conversation considerably less deep, but to young lovers, no less meaningful. They cooled the second beers in the lake, and enjoyed the warm, mosquito-free afternoon, and each other. By early evening, they'd eaten almost everything Pearl packed, and drank the last two beers. As they folded the blanket, still damp from the spring ground, Martin announced his decision.

"Pearl, it makes sense to enlist. I'm sure to be drafted, and I'll wind up God knows where. So then, where do I enlist? I still feel like Bloomer and Eagle Point are home. But I've met so many good people here, and I'm saving money, and I met a wonderful girl," Martin couldn't resist adding, "I'll introduce you to her sometime."

For all her popularity, Pearl was a private person, and revealed herself to others, even Martin, only in snippets. As Martin ran laughing to the roadster, he learned something about her he'd not known before; the part-time physical education teacher had a good arm. Her half-eaten apple caught him squarely in the back of the head.

Private Martin Treptow, 1917.
Courtesy of Cherokee Historical Society.

Chapter Twenty

When the various guard units were incorporated into the 42nd Division, regiments were increased in size. Each company would now have 250 men. By early July, the new American Expeditionary Force still lacked volunteers, both from regular army units and guard regiments. On July 20, 1917, America held its first draft lottery. Because of his age, his physical condition, and his lack of dependents, Martin knew that if he waited, he'd be a draftee and have no control over where he was sent. Instead, he enlisted in Company M of what became part of the 168th U.S. infantry.

The men reported for duty soon after, and within days boarded a train for Des Moines and the state fairgrounds. Enlistees arrived from around the state on August 20th, and only nine days later, with scarcely any drilling, the 168th marched in review for fairgoers. At the same time, Martin was putting his skills to work. While the unit was in Iowa, Everett McManus, one of the new company sergeants, wrote a letter home that was published in the *Semi-Weekly Democrat*. The letter read in part,

Treptow is barbering every day and has a chair. He gets out of detail and guard duty, and 10% of what he makes goes to the company mess fund

The fairgrounds barber shop didn't stay in operation long, however. Within a fortnight, arrangements were made to transfer to Camp Mills, New York. M Company traveled first to

Chicago, then Fort Wayne, then Buffalo, then Elmira, then Scranton, and ultimately to Garden City. Most of the men had shared farewells with loved ones at the depot in Cherokee, or at the fairgrounds in Des Moines. A few very fortunate ones were met in Garden City by relatives. Martin was thoroughly enjoying the new friendships made during the short encampment in Des Moines and the three-day trip to New York. He was absolutely ecstatic, however, to disembark from the train and see a smiling, more beautiful than ever, Pearl Van de Steeg.

"Pearl! My gosh, what are you doing here?"

"You asked me to come along, remember? Are you unhappy? Should I not be here?" She teased.

"I just--how?"

"Everyone in town knew where the 168th was going two weeks ago. Everett McManus--I told he's Sergeant McManus now--wrote a letter that was published in the Democrat. He said you even you had your own barber chair in Des Moines."

"I did, Pearl. I was making good money, too. But-how are you here?"

"Martin Treptow, I'm still not sure if you're happy about that…"

Martin lifted her off her feet and gave her a long kiss. Pearl seemed satisfied with the answer.

"I told them at the American and the Happy Hour they'd have to make do until you left for France. I found a room at a nice boarding house in New York, on Hopkinson Ave. I'm staying here as long as you are!"

"Oh my gosh, Pearl. I am so happy to…"

"Private!"

Sergeant McManus recognized Pearl immediately. "Ms. Van De Steeg, it's truly a delight to see you. Now, I must ask you to excuse the private for a moment. It seems the President has signed us up for a war, and the army requests the pleasure of Private Treptow's company."

Pearl had already written her address on a card. She slipped it into his pocket and added "I'll call for you tomorrow. If you can get free in the evening, please come see me." She sneaked in another kiss, and if Sergeant McManus noticed, he didn't let on.

The first night in camp was a blur. Private Treptow tried to keep his mind on organizing his uniform, rifle and equipment, but knowing Pearl had traveled so far from home just to see him left Martin more than a little distracted.

The men were assigned bunkmates, and Martin was happy to learn he'd be sharing a tent with Bill Klema. Bill was from Sutherland, and they got to know each other back at the fairgrounds. Bill had heard Martin bragging about his mother's cooking, and first thing they knew, they were sharing supper stories. Bill, too, was happy to have Martin for a bunkmate, but he worried a little, since Martin seemed particularly absent minded that first evening.

Chapter Twenty-One

As Martin and Bill unpacked and prepared their cots, some 20,000 pilgrims were heading back to their homes in Fatima, Portugal. That morning, in front of a huge crowd, three children claimed to have been visited by the Virgin Mary for the fifth time. According to the children, she told them, "Continue to pray the rosary, in order to obtain the end of the war."

Chapter Twenty-Two

Drilling commenced early the next morning. Martin and Bill answered reveille, emerged from their tent, and took in the neighborhood. Next to the 168th was the 167th Alabama. On the other side was the 166th Ohio. Next to Ohio was the 165th New York. The 167th and 165th went back a ways, so to speak. The 165th was formerly the 69th New York, and the 167th was once the 4th Alabama. They'd met at Bull Run and Fredericksburg, and rumor had it their acquaintance had been renewed at Camp Mills the evening of the 12th. As the men waited in line for morning mess, it sounded to Martin like another chapter was about to be written. Alabama and New York companies were on opposite sides of the mess tent, with Company M of the 168th in the middle. The taunts grew louder, and one of the Alabama men yelled, "Stand aside you farm boys, or we'll lick you, too!"

Just as it appeared the battle would be joined, a New York sergeant stepped in the middle of the Iowa ranks. He was slight of build and had what Martin's mother would call a baby face. He raised his arms, but otherwise stayed still and said nothing. This made the erstwhile combatants at least curious, and for a moment both sides stopped and stared at him. Then he spoke.

"My friends, why waste your energy today when there are no Huns among us? Friends from Alabama, we know how you fight. We are honored to go to war by your side. And you know how we fight. We charged Marys' Heights. You repelled us, and still we came. Trust me!" and his voice grew loader, "The Fighting Irish will always attack!" He was yelling now. "We'll fight together, until we have the Kaiser in a sack!"

Murmurs were heard. They became louder, and then some of the men of the 168th began to cheer. They were joined by the New York men, and just then, Martin heard his very first full-throated rebel yell. From that point on, any lingering animosity from the War Between the States was forgotten, and the 165th, the 167th, and the 168th trained and ultimately fought as one.

Martin was close to the front of the line, and it was long, but no one complained when the young sergeant asked to cut in front of him.

"Sergeant, that was very impressive. How did you manage that?"

"Actually, private, I surprised myself. I watched the brawling last night and vowed to say something this morning if it continued. Fighting among ourselves seems to me to be a tremendous waste of energy. And it's sinful."

Martin smiled. "The great multitudes came to him, and he healed them."

"Well, private, do I condemn your blasphemy, comparing me to our Savior, or do I applaud your knowledge of the Gospel of Matthew?"

"Didn't mean to blaspheme, sergeant. The passage just came to my mind."

"Well then, I'll applaud. Where'd you learn of the word of God?"

"My mother read Bible stories to us when I was little. As I got older, I read the Bible myself. I still do."

"Well, perhaps if everyone did as you do, we wouldn't be preparing to kill our fellow man. What's your name, private?"

"Treptow, Martin Treptow. They call me Trep."

"I'm pleased to meet you, Private Treptow. I'm Sergeant Kilmer. If we should meet again, and no officers are looking on, you may call me Joyce. Now eat a hearty breakfast and train hard. Before you know it, we'll be in France."

Sergeant Kilmer was pleased to have met a fellow student of the Word, and truth be told, he expected the men of the prairie to be a little more roughhewn. He also had to admit he was surprised by the success of his impromptu speech. Playing his words back in his mind, he liked the sound of "the Kaiser in a sack," and made note of it. He also thought "Fighting Irish" had a nice ring.

The following weeks were given to constant drilling-marching, marksmanship, bayonet drills-and preparing to move tons of materiel across the ocean. On Sunday, September 23rd, the Secretary of War, Newton Baker reviewed the Rainbow Division. Several days later, the 168th was visited and reviewed by Governor Harding and Iowa's two senators.

The pace was steady, but the routine soon became monotonous. The saving grace was the liberal issuance of passes to leave the base in the evenings. Soldiers flocked to taverns in the nearby towns of Forest Hills, Flushing, Hempstead and Jamaica. Other evenings were given to nights in New York, where some of the boys became men for the price of a month's pay.

For Martin, every trip off the base meant a visit with Pearl. If they didn't go to dinner or see a movie, they'd have dinner with the owners of the boarding house, then walk the neighborhood, or maybe just sit on the steps. One warm fall evening as they relaxed on the stoop, the owner asked if they'd like their picture taken. Pearl initially demurred; "Martin, look at my hair. It's all over. And I'm wearing my old black button up shoes. At least let me run inside and brush my hair and put on my opera pumps."

"Pearl, you are absolutely beautiful, and you would be just as beautiful wearing a snood and skis. And look at me – I'm half in uniform! Now sit, and let the man take our picture."

The owner took several shots and promised them prints as soon as they were developed.

On Monday, October 8th, the 168th received orders to prepare to ship out. The men assumed they had at least another week, but no one could be sure, so virtually the entire regiment asked for passes for the evening of the 9th.

Martin was shining his boots when Bill and a group of Company M men converged on him.

"Trep, we're going to McSorley's in the city. Every man shipping out gets a free turkey and ale dinner. When we get done, we hang a wishbone in the rafters to reclaim when we get back home. Come with us, it might be the last night on this side of the water for a while."

"Thanks, fellas. I appreciate the offer, and I agree it might be our last night, so I'm headed over to see Pearl."

"Tell you what, Trep," said Bill. "You hang a wishbone in her rafters for us, and we'll hang one at McSorley's for you."

Bill ducked just in time to avoid the flying boot.

McSorley's Bar. New York City. 2020 WWI wishbones in the rafters, *Courtesy of Jake Butter.*

Chapter Twenty-Three

For a long time, Martin and Pearl were content to hold hands on the boardinghouse steps and watch the stars. When the street was completely quiet, Pearl stood up and said, "Martin, wait here. I have something for you." Pearl went to her room and returned several minutes later.

"This is for you, Martin. I want you to keep this with you at all times."

Pearl handed him a photograph of herself. Martin turned it over and read the inscription on the back "with all the love in the world for Trep."

"Trep? I thought you didn't like Trep."

"You told me Trep was earnest and strong. You're going to war, and you're going to be the most earnest, and absolutely the strongest American soldier in France. Trep is going to war. Martin is staying here with me until Trep returns."

They shared smiles, and Martin asked for a pen. "I need to add something to make this perfect." Below Pearl's inscription, Martin wrote, "In case of accident, please send this picture to my sweetheart, Box 222 Cherokee, Iowa."

Martin didn't realize when he added the postscript that Pearl would focus on the first four words. She was fighting not to cry, and not really succeeding. He took her hands in his, and said softly, "Pearl, I'll be okay. I promise."

"I don't have any metaphors, Martin. Please come home safely, please come home."

"I promise. Trep will be just fine. I have to come back to you, Pearl. You're my strongest branch." And at that they both smiled a little.

"There is something I've wanted to ask you before I ship out. Remember that song back at the farmer's picnic – when you sang real slow? Did you sing that for me?"

"Martin, you promise to come home, and I promise I'll tell you then. Do we have a deal?"

"We have a deal. I love you, Pearl. I promise I'll come home."

Martin Treptow · Pearl Van De Steeg

Martin and Pearl, 1917. Pearl's boarding house at 209 Hopkinson Ave., now Thomas S. Boyland St. New York, New York. *Courtesy of Sanford Museum, Cherokee, Iowa.*

Chapter Twenty-Four

We wake at four in the morning

With the Buglers raising Hell

And the officers start a yelling

Like they had garden truck to sell.

They yank off all your blankets, and give your head a shove,
and bellow in your sleepy ear, "crawl out and get above."

Life on the President Grant

Anonymous

In 1861, Edward J. Harland and Gustav W. Wolff established a ship building enterprise in Belfast. By the end of the 19th century, the company was one of the world's premiere ship builders. On February 19, 1903, Harland & Wolff christened and launched the *SS Servian*, built for a subsidiary of J.P. Morgan's International Mercantile Marine Company. Harland & Wolff employed the best designers and engineers, and their products were considered technological marvels. In fact, six years later, the same company laid the keel for a fantastic new passenger ship, the *RMS Titanic*.

The *Servian* was originally intended for the North Atlantic cargo market, but shortly after she was christened, her owners deemed the plan unprofitable, and in 1907 sold the ship to the Hamburg-American Packet Steamship Company. Then war broke out in 1914 and flagged at the time as a German merchant ship, she remained docked at harbor in Hoboken, New Jersey. In 1917, she was commissioned as a U.S. Navy transport. When it purchased the vessel, the Hamburg-American Company renamed the ship the *President Grant*, a former commander-in-chief remembered as surly, unattractive, and unconcerned with the comforts of his men. Subsequent events would prove the moniker apt.

The men had known since late September they'd soon be leaving for France. One of their commanders, Lieutenant Colonel Tinley had sailed on September 23rd, and the October 8th order came as no surprise. On October 16th, Martin learned that new U.S. government regulations provided life insurance policies for all soldiers headed to the front. He completed his application, naming his sister as beneficiary, and spent the next day packing to leave. On the morning of the 18th, the men rode the train to ferries which took them down the East River, around the southern point of Manhattan Island, and up the North River to Hoboken. Over the next few hours, the 168th infantry and seven other units boarded the *President Grant* and found their berths in the lower decks. At 9:30 p.m. the ship left the dock and headed for the North Atlantic.

The voyage would be talked about for decades. The ship had sat at the dock for several years, and she'd never been property reconditioned before filling her hold with soldiers. The vessel was originally designed to hold 1200 passengers, but nearly 5,000 men were crammed into the space. There was no room for a proper mess hall, and meals were reduced from three to two per day. Freshwater became a premium, and the sailors maintaining the ship began to black market jugs and bottles to the soldiers. Two days into the trip, Martin asked the M Company clerk, tasked to document the voyage, what he'd written so far. The handwriting was barely legible, befitting a scribe coping with rough seas. It read simply, "A wild nightmare... something too unsavory, too unpleasant to be real."

After several days at sea, they encountered a storm, and hundreds of the men, many who had never been on any ship, much less a trans-Atlantic vessel, became violently ill. Heads overflowed or malfunctioned, which forced the passengers to improvise. The company clerk wrote, "In a short time the sanitary condition of the between decks became unspeakable... in order to escape the fetid quarters allotted them, the men resorted to all manner of connivance to remain on deck at night, secreting themselves in lifeboats, in the piles of baggage heaped about, or in any other shelter where they could avoid the vigilant eye of the sentry."

The *President Grant* also had slowed significantly since the start of the voyage. Four days after leaving the states, she was less than 900 miles from New York, and averaging only four knots per hour. The ship was part of a convoy that included other transports, two destroyers, and an armored cruiser. The glacial pace of the ship was now slowing the entire small flotilla. Ultimately, the decision was made to return the ship to New York, and on the evening of October 27th, the vessel again docked in Hoboken.

By late evening, the 168th had gotten off the ship and boarded a train back to Camp Mills. Most units had broken camp by that time, and the tents were in shambles. Martin described the conditions of that first night in a letter to a friend.

> *The night that we got back here at the islands again it was raining something fierce. Thunder just pierced through us. The only time we could see was where it would be lightning.*

We hiked in mud up to our ankles all the way, about two miles. For about two blocks we waded through water up to our knees. Got in camp about 1:30a.m., had to sleep on the wet ground until a.m. reveille.

The men were left to find shelter wherever they could. After several days of relying upon the charity of other units, most notably the 167th Alabama, the men began scavenging the abandoned camps. On October 29th, Sergeant Kilmer and the rest of the 165th moved out, and the Iowa boys moved into their quarters. On Monday, November 13th, orders were received to be ready for an early start the next morning. Long before daybreak the next day, the First and Third Battalions, the Headquarters Company, and the Supply Company boarded the train for Long Island City, then transferred at the Chelsea Docks. The Third Battalion boarded the *R.M.S. Celtic* of the White Star Line at Pier 60. They again passed the Statue of Liberty and anchored in the lower bay. On the evening of November 14th, the ships headed into open ocean.

They sailed first for Halifax, then joined a convoy headed toward England. On November 26th, at the entrance to the Irish Sea, a periscope was sighted, but it soon disappeared, and nothing came of it. That evening, the ships docked at Belfast, and the Iowa soldiers spent Thanksgiving aboard ship in the harbor.

The *Celtic* and the *Aurania* left Belfast on the 30th and anchored at Liverpool on December 1st. On the 8th, the unit took a train to Southampton, and the next day, three ships carrying the 168th Iowa arrived at Le Havre. The trains headed straight toward Paris, and the men excitedly looked forward to seeing the Eiffel Tower and the Arc de Triomphe. But the train never stopped, instead heading some 300 kilometers east and south to the village of Rimaucourt. From December 12th, the day they arrived, they trained almost nonstop. Unlike the disorganized first attempts back at the fairgrounds, and the more orderly but still hypothetical war drilling at Camp Mills, the men knew this was much more serious business. In mid-February 1918, the 168th was ordered north, to relieve a French division in the trenches. Martin, however, would not make the trip.

Chapter Twenty-Five

On February 3rd, Martin awoke with a sore throat. It got worse through the day, and by that evening, he'd developed a fever. The next day he noticed a rash on his neck that looked like sunburn. On Tuesday, February 5th, the big story in camp was the American pilot, Stephen Thompson, who'd shot down a German plane. Word also spread that a German U-boat had sunk the *Tuscania,* a British steamship carrying 2000 young American soldiers, including most of the Chippewa County, Wisconsin National Guard unit. Over 200 lost their lives, but among the survivors was a strong swimmer from Cameron, John Henry Cook.

Martin paid little attention to the stories. The rash had spread to his arms and legs and a medic recognized the signs of scarlet fever. He was sent to the 168th aid station, and later, as the fever continued to rise, to the division hospital. Neither the fever nor the rash subsided, and the doctors feared it would spread to his kidneys. His fluids were monitored, and he was ordered to remain bedridden. It wasn't until late February that the fever broke, and although Martin was still relegated to the base hospital, he felt well enough to write in his journal, and respond to the pile of letters from home, most of which came from Pearl.

Martin started keeping a journal when the 168th left for Des Moines, and he tried to write every day. From his hospital bed, he looked back over the entries and wasn't satisfied with what he'd written. He procured a clean ledger book from the YMCA, and over the next few weeks, he edited and revised. He was particularly displeased with what little he'd written on New

Year's Eve: "The end of a long journey. Now bring on your wars." When he reached December 31st in the revised journal, he included a promise he'd made to himself months earlier and had jotted down on the last page of the original notebook.

Chapter Twenty-Six

By the first week of March, Martin felt fine, and had it been up to him, he'd rejoin his unit. However, the doctors were still restricting his activity and keeping a close watch on liquid in-liquid out. Martin suggested that if the army needed a pee officer, he'd immediately seek the commission. By mid-month, Martin couldn't be kept down, and his doctors reluctantly allowed him to help with hospital chores. He began by assisting the orderlies, and by the third week, he was unloading rail cars. On Saturday, March 23rd, he sought permission to travel to a depot just outside Paris, to help unload supplies. There had been an unusual influenza outbreak at Brest, one of the debarkation ports, and the resulting transfer of hospital-assigned manpower to the coast left a need for help at Nogent-sur-Marne. To his great delight, Martin was granted not only leave to assist, but a three-day pass on the back end to visit Paris. Martin arose early the next morning to prepare a bag and pack his dress uniform.

He'd spent the last 48 hours preparing beds for an anticipated influx of casualties from the 165th New York. They began arriving early Sunday morning, the 24th. To Martin's great surprise, accompanying the wounded soldiers was someone he had not seen since Camp Mills, none other than Sergeant Kilmer.

Martin jumped to his feet. "Sergeant Kilmer! Why are you here? Were you wounded?"

"No, thank God. Colonel Donovan asked me to accompany the wounded back behind the lines. Apparently just the sight of me lifts their spirits."

Martin didn't need to see to see the eye roll to know what the sergeant thought of the plan.

"I'm entitled to spend all of 24 hours here, and then they're sending me to Paris, to meet the French literati. Trep, this is not why I enlisted. But the colonel promised me a transfer to intelligence as soon as I return to the front, if I made this trip. So here I am."

"Sergeant Kilmer…"

"Joyce. Please."

"Joyce, they're sending me to Nogent-sur-Marne to unload materials, and then I have three days to myself in Paris. Perhaps we'll see each other."

"Trep, let's do better than that. I'll accompany you to the supply depot and actually help the war effort. I'll tell my French liaison to meet us at one of the railway stations the next day in Paris. Trep, I just learned another poem was accepted for publication. You can help me celebrate. We'll explore the city, and we'll ask our liaison to direct us to a fine restaurant. Are you game?"

"I sure am! Sergeant …Joyce, that'd be mighty fine!"

The army had different ideas. Sergeant Alfred Joyce Kilmer would not be working at a supply depot, where he might be photographed working alongside colored soldiers. So they altered their plans. Martin would stay at the supply depot the evening of the 24th and meet Joyce and his French liaison at the Gare du Nord station early the next morning.

Joyce was waiting for Martin as he stepped off the train. He was accompanied by a rather stern looking young French officer.

Martin reflexively began to salute, but instead, Joyce extended his hand.

"Private Martin Treptow, I'd like you to meet Lieutenant Marcel Bouchard."

Lieutenant Bouchard stood ramrod straight. "Private Treptow."

"Martin, Lieutenant Bouchard is going to show me his city, with you as my special guest. And tomorrow the Paris patriciate shall be meeting none other than Joyce Kilmer, the world-famous poet."

Lieutenant Bouchard missed the sarcasm entirely. Martin guessed the nuance exceeded his English, or perhaps the lieutenant was just accustomed to people who said things like that and actually meant it.

Sergeant Kilmer continued, "I have a request, Lieutenant. Today, we are tourists, being shown the city by a proud resident, who is a new friend. I am Joyce, this is Trep, and I would prefer that you'd be Marcel."

For the first time the lieutenant smiled. Then he extended his hand. "Trep, Joyce… I'm Marcel. Let me show you my city."

Marcel immediately launched into the role of tour guide. "Before we leave the square, please appreciate the facade of the Gare du Nord. The building was completed in 1864, as part of Haussmann's--you are familiar with Haussmann—his modernization of the city. The statues at the crown of the building were intended to give it a classic appearance.

"We shall walk to the Arc de Triomphe, then to the Trocadero and down the Champs du Mars, then back across the

117

Seine to the Place de la Concorde, and eventually to the restaurant I've selected for us. It's a rather long walk, but we can stop as often as you'd like, wherever you'd like."

The men turned right on Rue Lafayette and headed west toward the Arc de Triomphe. The street was wide, but the uniform multistory buildings on both sides made Martin feel like he was walking in a canyon. It reminded him of his trips into Manhattan with Pearl, and for just a moment, he forgot that he was half a world away from her. Soon they came to a city park on their right, and Marcel again was the knowledgeable host.

"This is Square Montholon. It was designed by Baron Haussmann's engineer, Jean Charles Alphand at the time of your Civil War. The wrought iron fence surrounding the park dates from the time of Louis Phillipe. The bronze sculpture in the middle is called *l'Ours, l'Aigle, et le Vautour*...The Bear, the Eagle and the Vulture."

Martin was having the time of his life. He'd wanted to see Paris since he was a boy, and from the very moment he enlisted, he'd hoped to visit the City of Light. He also was devouring every syllable of Marcel's narrative. Joyce was less enthralled. He was enjoying the walk and made mental notes of the sights and sounds of the city. But he was unaccustomed to playing the role of follower.

When they reached Boulevard Haussmann, Joyce suggested it might be a good time to stop for an early lunch. They'd walked barely a mile and a half, but the march had been anything but double quick. Marcel paused frequently to explain the sights of Rue Lafayette, and just when they resumed their pace, Martin would stop them with a question. Joyce felt like he was squiring an inquisitive puppy; he half expected Martin to lift his leg on a hitching post. It was almost noon when they reached the avenue that would lead them to the Arc de Triomphe.

Marcel responded enthusiastically. "This would be a splendid time, and I know the perfect spot. *On y va!*" The three soldiers turned slightly left, onto Rue Haling, rather than right onto Boulevard Haussmann. In fifty meters, they found themselves in the Place de l'Opera.

"My friends, welcome inside the beating heart of Paris."

Martin couldn't believe he'd not heard or sensed the plaza from blocks away. The square was a beehive of carriages and taxis and bicycles and busses, moving every direction at once. A mustachioed policeman stood in the center of the street in front of a fantastic edifice, waving his white baton. Pedestrians darting in and out reminded him of the polliwogs back in Popple Lake in the spring, scurrying in all directions to avoid the bass fingerlings.

"What's the building with the gold top?" Martin asked Marcel.

"At the cafe I'll tell you all about it. For now, keep your eyes on the taxis and carriages, and keep your feet out of the horse shit."

And across the square they went, three little tadpoles in the human pond that was Place de l'Opera.

Marcel's destination was the *Café de la Paix*, where the Boulevard des Capucines meets the square. Martin and Joyce could not have distinguished it from a dozen other sidewalk restaurants they passed that day. Marcel's broad smile, however, told them this was no ordinary cafe.

119

"My friends, welcome to the café of Emile Zola and Guy Maupassant, and the favored haunt of Edward, Prince of Wales. It will be an honor for us to merely be seen here." And to Marcel's absolute delight, they found a street side table.

"Now let me tell you about that grand structure, Private Trep. I'm sure you've never read *The Phantom of the Opera*?"

"I have."

"I'm surprised. It's not widely known."

 Martin smiled. "I read."

"So you do. Well, Leroux used this building, the *Palais Garnier*, as his setting. Garnier was the architect. Napoleon III chose his design over two hundred others."

"Is that gold at the top?"

"It's gilded bronze, and the figures at the top, *L'Harmoine* and *La Poesie* are gilded copper."

Joyce smiled. "Harmony, and I believe I know the other one."

"I would have been disappointed had you'd not known that, my friend. Now Trep, look to the center at the top of the structure. That's Apollo, and the figures on each side are guarded by Pegasus. Now observe the columns on the second level. There are sculptures of the great composers in each space. Beethoven and Mozart are near the center.

"Trep, someday you must tour this wonderful building. You've never seen an interior so grand. And the acoustics! Mon Dieu! An ordinary pianist will sound like Chopin. Musicians truly worthy of the stage make music that's never forgotten. When you return, and you must return, bring with you someone very special. If you're in love, you will fall in love all over again."

Suddenly Martin was back in the third row of the American Theatre, thoroughly enjoying a certain pianist eminently worthy of the stage. If God allowed him to return to visit this marvelous building, he knew exactly the "someone very special" who'd accompany him.

The soldiers were in no hurry to leave the easy ambience of the café, and even Joyce, who rarely drank (and who Martin suspected of favoring temperance) accepted Marcel's offer of an absinthe before they resumed their journey. They backtracked to the junction of Rue Lafayette and Avenue Haussmann, then turned left toward the Arc de Triomphe. The street was not as wide as Rue Lafayette and Martin asked why the street named after the architect of modern Paris was so narrow.

"Not everyone in the government approved of Haussmann's changes, or what they were costing," Marcel explained, "He was fired in 1870. Fortunately, his plans continued to be carried out. The Opera we just passed-it was completed in 1875. This boulevard will be widened when we defeat the Boche."

"What will happen after the war?" Joyce asked, as much to himself as to his comrades. "Will there be a Franco-Prussian alliance some day?"

Marcel bristled at the suggestion. "Ally with the Huns? Never! They will always seek to conquer, and we will always be on our guard, and we will never forget!"

Up to now, Martin was quiet. "May I ask you a question, Lieutenant?"

"Private...Trep...you may ask me anything."

"Well, Lieutenant...Marcel...the French people I've met seem to have their own special hatred for the Huns. Something that seems to come from deeper down than just the current war. I've always enjoyed reading about European history, and Charlemagne. I thought the French and Germans were brethren. I thought England was your enemy, or at least your bitter rival."

"Trep, Modern England is not the British Empire of the 1700's. As our nations modernize, we share more goals. The German states are not ghosts of the Holy Roman Empire. Remember, Cain and Abel were brethren as well.

"Let me tell you a story. Fifty years ago, along this very street, was the most famous steakhouse of Paris – the *Boucherie Anglaise.*

"On Christmas day, 1870, the menu featured *Consommé d'elephant.* The fare may have been exotic, but the source was hardly so. Paris was besieged since September 19th, and Parisians were running out of food. Butchers had featured equine cuts for months as the war raged. As Paris became surrounded, however, even horse meat became scarce, and eventually, dogs, cats and even rats disappeared from the city streets. Chefs were challenged to be increasingly more creative, and by November the Jockey Club featured *Salmi de Rat a la Robert.*

"Inevitably, hungry Parisians and resourceful quisiniers turned their palates to the Paris zoos. For a price, zookeepers obligingly parted with the herbivores, and later, the wolves and bears. It wasn't until December, however, that the city's beloved elephants, Castor and Pollux -- known to all the children of the city -- were sold. Their slaughter was a sad conclusion to a year in which our armies suffered 300,000 casualties, and Napoleon III surrendered at Sedan.

"Conditions deteriorated from very bad to much, much worse. In early January, bread was rationed, and by mid-month, the Prussians began lobbing artillery shells into the city. On January 28th, Paris surrendered, and five weeks later, the Prussians held a victory parade.

"Paris actually was occupied for only a matter of days, and when they left, the children scrubbed the streets to remove the stench. The stigma of defeat was more difficult to purge. There will always be a next time with le Boche, and we will never forget."

Martin and Joyce stayed silent as the three men resumed their walk. Finally, they reached the Arc de Triomphe. They'd walked the length of Avenue Haussmann, and Marcel suggested they stop for a glass of wine.

"More wine? It's barely afternoon?"

"Monsieur Kilmer try to be a Parisian for one day. In my professional opinion, as an officer and a Parisian, I recommend wine."

A glance at Martin told Joyce he was outvoted.

"There's a wonderful brasserie just a block or so away, on Avenue George V." Soon the three found themselves at Fouquet's, enjoying a bottle selected by Marcel, and watching the passersby. It was a beautiful spring day, and during those periods where no soldiers or aid workers passed by, the three could imagine a Paris without war. They finished their wine, and Marcel paid the bill. They retreated back up the broad avenue, turned left on Avenue Kleber, and walked to the Place du Trocadero.

Marcel continued to be the tour host. "The place is named in honor of the Battle of Trocadero, in which the French army helped the Bourbon monarchy put down a liberal rebellion in Spain. The palais was built for the 1878 World's Fair."

Martin looked across the Siene to the Eiffel Tower, and the broad expanse of the Champs du Mars. There was not a cloud in the sky, and the picture was everything and more than he'd ever imagined. Even the urbane Joyce was caught up in the moment. They presented their Kodaks to Marcel and stood with the famous edifice as the backdrop. They smiled for their photographer, and then the three descended the hill and crossed the bridge to the structure itself.

More pictures were taken under the metal legs. Martin knew his father would be impressed by the engineering, and he imagined Joyce would wax appropriately poetic about the simple symmetry of the great skeleton. He wasn't sure, however, if Joyce could find a perfect rhyme for superstructure.

Having observed the tower from every angle imaginable, they walked along the Champs du Mars to where a small crowd was watching a military band. As they grew nearer, Martin recognized the uniforms as American, and Joyce seized the opportunity to be *au courant*.

"They're the Hellfighters, the 369th Infantry jazz band. The conductor is James Reese Europe, the leader of the Clef Club Orchestra. They were one of the first jazz bands to perform at

Carnegie Hall. The Clef Club may be the most famous jazz band in America."

The band was between songs at that moment, and then the band leader said, "You know me and the boys belong to the 93rd, and the rest of the gang are at the front. I'd like to play for you a new song about what we're doing out there. It's called '*On Patrol in No Man's Land.*'"

It took Martin a minute to comprehend what Joyce and Marcel already knew. The orchestra was all Negroes, part of the black infantry unit he'd been hearing about. When the song ended, and the applause died down, Martin posed a question to Joyce.

"You know, for two days at the supply depot I worked alongside darkies. They were darn good workers, and strong to a man. And boy, they make some great music. But can they fight?"

Joyce responded immediately. "They're not 'darkies', Trep, and they're not 'niggers.' And you wonder whether Negroes can fight? Have you heard of the 54th Massachusetts? They were freedmen and former slaves who fought in the Civil War. Their unit was highly decorated, and they suffered horrific casualties at Fort Pillow. I have no doubt that when given the chance the 93rd infantry will exhibit the same bravery."

Now Marcel spoke. "Your American generals and your American president refuse to allow you to fight alongside these Negroes. We French have no such prejudices. Private Trep, when the war comes to you, you would prefer the man next to you in the trench be white?"

"Marcel, when the war comes to me, I hope the man next to me knows how to handle a rifle, that he'll fight, and that he'll protect my hind end. If he can do that, he can be black or white or French or British or Scottish…" then he nodded to Joyce, "or even a poet."

The good weather was holding, and the three were in no hurry to leave. The orchestra eventually moved on from the military and patriotic songs to more modern music. Martin wondered if Marcel would object to a military band playing jazz and ragtime, but he noticed the lieutenant nodding his head, snapping his fingers and tapping his feet, as close to dancing as a man could be while standing still. The band finished the next song and adjusted their sheet music. They then launched into a rousing rendition of "*Alexander's Ragtime Band*". Joyce and Marcel smiled and mouthed the words, but Martin was 4,500 miles away, watching the prettiest girl in Cherokee sing just it for him.

A couple songs later, Marcel suggested they head in the general direction of where they would dine, and Joyce agreed. Martin was still at the farmer's picnic, and his companions noticed his thoughts were far from the Champs du Mars.

"Dreaming about your Heloise, my friend?" Marcel teased. "Do you know the story?"

Martin again caught Marcel by surprise. "Of course, I do. Heloise and Abelard were twelfth century lovers. Heloise was the niece of a Notre Dame church elder. When her uncle realized how intelligent she was, he sought out Abelard, one of the city's great intellectuals. Heloise was twenty years younger than Abelard, but teacher and student fell in love, and failed to hide their relationship. Abelard was attacked and castrated by ruffians hired by Heloise's' uncle. Realizing they could not consummate their love, they agreed to take holy orders. Abelard became a monk, and Heloise joined a convent. Their passion for each other did not abate, however, and their letters have survived."

"I'm very impressed. Do you also know where they are buried?' Marcel asked.

"I do not."

"Six centuries after their deaths, Josephine Bonaparte ordered their remains to be entombed together at Pere Lachaise. Shortly after began the tradition of lovers visiting the tomb and sometimes leaving messages for a loved one far distant."

"Is Pere Lachaise in the city?"

"It is. You can walk there."

"I'll be sure to visit their tombs. And yes, I was thinking of my Heloise. I hope to see her again... without the need to be castrated."

Chapter Twenty-Seven

They left the Champs du Mars and walked along the Avenue de Tourville to the Invalides, then to the Quai d'Orsay, and crossed the river again at Pont de la Concorde. They skirted the large square, and Marcel showed the Americans the site of the guillotine. They turned on the Rue de Rivoli and Marcel explained that the wide avenue had been a pet project of French leaders since the time of Napoleon.

When they reached Rue de Castiglione, Marcel said, "We turn here," and they entered Place Vendome. Martin immediately focused his gaze on the obelisk in the center of the square, topped by a statue who he guessed to be Napoleon. The structure was hugged by sandbags to a height of perhaps 20 feet. Martin assumed they were placed there to protect the edifice from shelling. He'd noticed similar battlements in front of the Palais Garnier. Before he could question Marcel, however, the lieutenant directed his gaze elsewhere.

"Look to the left, gentlemen. It's not an old hotel, but a fine hotel, with an excellent restaurant, overseen by one of the world's greatest chefs. Joyce, you asked me to select a fine restaurant to finish your day in the city, and to celebrate the publication of your latest poem. I think you'll be pleased."

Martin and Joyce turned to look at the hotel. They saw no hint of wartime depravation. Doormen on each side of the ornate entry stood at perfect, motionless attention. The carriages in front of the entrance were clean and polished. Even the horses seemed to exude an aristocratic air. But for the expensive motorcars nearby, the scene evoked the apex of *la Belle Epoque.*

All three soldiers were wearing dress uniforms, but as they approached the steps Martin couldn't help but wonder if they were appropriately appointed for such a place. But if they were underdressed, the doormen didn't show it.

"*Bonsoir, Messieurs,*" and then in English, "Welcome to the Ritz. Will you be dining with us tonight?"

This time, Joyce tried his French. "*Oui, s'il vous plait. Le Jardin.*"

Another employee of the hotel, impeccably dressed, with perfect posture and a measured gait that would impress Pershing himself, led them down the long hallway to the restaurant. Martin had never seen such a place. The hall was lushly carpeted, and Martin figured that each painting probably cost more than his parents' home. The soldiers were directed to the rear of the restaurant, although center tables were open. Joyce wondered if the Maitre'd had deliberately tried to keep the war away from the other diners. Martin, on the other hand, was quite content to see everything and watch everyone.

Martin wondered how the employee who was seating people could wait on them as well. The answer came shortly, in the person of another young man who brought them a pitcher of water. As Martin was pondering just how many people worked here, yet another waiter brought their menus.

"You won't believe how I've looked forward to real food." Martin said. "Marcel, could you translate for me? I'm a meat and potatoes man, so suggest a meal I might like."

"Trep, my friend, one does not simply 'order a meal' here. One of the world's great chefs, Auguste Escoffier, created everything on the menu. He believes that your pairings-your meat, your sauces, your vegetables, and yes, your potatoes-should be left to your individual choice. He calls it '*a la carte.*' Dining is like making love, Private Trep. There will be a first course to tease and tempt your palate. You will desire more. And the combinations of delights for the main course are virtually unlimited."

Joyce was not comfortable with such talk. "That's not how I make love," Joyce responded, "and my wife has given me five children."

Marcel winked at Martin. "Perhaps if you had, my friend, she would have given you seven."

"Alright Marcel, so what do I order to tease and tempt?" Martin asked.

"I recommend the escargots. I'm sure Escoffier will have created a coulis that will be memorable."

"And what is escargots?" Martin asked.

Martin missed the exchange of smiles between his companions. "It is a national secret that I cannot share until you try it for yourself." Marcel responded.

He then translated the remainder of the menu for Martin, and for Joyce, who grudgingly admitted he did not understand all the words. A slight young Anamese appeared at their table to refill the water pitcher. He greeted them with a smile, and Martin began to give the man his order.

"He's just here to refill your water glass. The waiter will take our orders", Joyce informed him.

Just then, a fourth person appeared at their table, Joyce's subtle shake of the head told Martin not to give his order to this man, either. He asked if they preferred wine, and Marcel accepted the sommelier's suggestion. Finally, the waiter appeared, and took their orders.

They relaxed and enjoyed the wine. Martin had never been a big drinker; unless he was famished, he liked to take his time and appreciate how the first taste of alcohol seemed to smooth life's rough edges. The men said little, now comfortable with being the only uniformed diners. After a time the waiter appeared with their first course. Martin couldn't believe his eyes. "Jesus! These are snails! Where's my escargots?"

Marcel and Joyce's laughter drew the attention of the other diners. "Martin, just try one," Marcel suggested.

Martin picked gingerly at one of the huge snails, paused briefly, took a breath, and popped it into his mouth whole. He paused for a moment, and said, "These aren't bad. Snails! Good heavens, what will my mother think? Marcel, you're right about the sauce. It's not too strong, but just…. Joyce, give me a word."

"Sublime?" Joyce offered.

"Sublime. Yes, sublime."

Soon, despite Marcel's pleas that they savor and discuss every bite, the Americans' hunger, and simply their excitement over a civilized meal overcame any need to maintain the conversation. They ate and drank, smiled and nodded, and enjoyed their best meal in months. When they finished, the waiter suggested a special dessert, "created by Escoffier himself." Shortly after, three small ice sculpted swans appeared, each containing a concoction of peaches and cream. "Monsieur

Escoffier calls this Peche Melba. I'm sure you will enjoy it." The waiter said.

"Joyce, Trep—you are familiar with The Swan? The dessert is named after her."

Joyce seized the opportunity to enlighten Martin. "Nellie Melba is an Australian opera singer. Some consider her the finest soprano of *la Belle Epoque.*"

"I know a beautiful soprano who would enjoy that story, and this desert. If I only had my kodak, I would take a picture for her", said Martin.

"Again, your Heloise. She seems never far from your heart."

Marcel had intended the comment as a little joke, but two bottles of wine elicited a different response. All three men grew quiet, and for a few moments thought about those who were never far from their hearts.

They finished their desserts and a third bottle of wine. By now most of the other diners had finished, and the soldiers were nearly alone in the beautiful, cavernous room. As they sat contented, the Anamese appeared to take their plates. He looked at Martin and Joyce and smiled. "Welcome to the American soldiers." Martin noticed his accent differed from English-speaking Frenchmen, and Joyce thought he detected a trace of sarcasm.

"Thank you. It was a wonderful dinner." responded Martin.

The man was a colonial. Marcel guessed perhaps an Indochinese. He smiled, and the men noted that he had much better teeth than most of his countrymen. He also was unusually self-confident for a colonial; not at all obsequious.

He then spoke to Marcel directly, this time in French. Marcel looked at Martin. "He wants to know why you are here."

"I came for a fine meal."

"No, he means what brought you here as a soldier. Why did you decide to fight?"

The question caught Martin by surprise. "When America joined the war, we were asked to serve. I answered the call, and I'm serving my country."

The server and Marcel spoke again, and Marcel asked Martin, "He wants to know if you've made a pledge. He understands all Americans have been asked to make a pledge: a children's pledge, a housewives' pledge, a farmers' pledge. He wants to know if you have made a pledge."

"Tell him I've pledged to go home in one piece," Martin responded with a smile.

Marcel relayed the response to the server and another question was posed. "He wants to know why America is here."

"Well we don't go spoiling for a fight," Martin responded, somewhat defensively.

Marcel and the server spoke again, and Marcel said, "He means why America decided to join the war?"

Martin had no immediate answer. He thought for a moment, and began slowly, "I'm not the President, so I can't speak for him or Congress. I think France and the Allies asked for help, and we responded." He paused again. "Germany doesn't belong in your country."

The young man raised his eyebrows, and he posed another question through Marcel. "He asks if America will stay after the war."

"Our job is to help win the war. When it's won we'll go home."

The man grew more excited, and asked a question directly, in English. "What if the Communards attempt another revolution? Will you interfere?"

"I guess that's not our decision. A country has the right to govern itself as it sees fit," responded Martin.

Marcel and the busboy then engaged in a longer, more animated discussion. Their voices grew louder, and Joyce asked – more to quiet them – what they were discussing.

The busboy responded directly to Joyce, again in English. "I asked him when France would allow Indochina to govern itself."

"Is that really something Indochina is ready for? "Joyce asked.

"Were the American colonies ready in 1776? I have lived in Boston. I know your history. You were 2 million farmers and a thousand aristocrats, most of whom were Tories! We are as ready as you were, and we have the right to govern ourselves, just as you Americans claimed that right."

The busboy stared at the three of them, and no one spoke. He then nodded and exhibited the smile of someone who knows they've proven a point, and left the room with their plates. The soldiers had not anticipated such a serious discussion, especially after three bottles of wine.

Marcel spoke first. "A waiter should not even be speaking to guests in that manner. He knows nothing. They come here and make no attempt to understand our culture or assimilate. And the ones with half a brain – like that fellow – do nothing but stir up trouble!"

Now Joyce spoke. "But of course, you French have no such prejudices."

Joyce's flippant comment only increased the tension, and when the bill was paid, Martin suggested they walk outside and enjoy the spring evening. That seemed to help, and the conversation became more convivial as they made their way back to the hotel. Martin was curious, though, about what Joyce thought about his responses to the busboy.

"Joyce, did you agree with my answers to the colonial's questions?" Martin asked.

"I did" Joyce responded. "And now I'm pondering my pledge."

The streets were dark. Martin could not see Joyce's eyes, nor did his tone provide any hint as to whether he was serious. Joyce, however, could see Martin's face in the streetlight, and he wondered why his friend was smiling.

Ritz Paris 1910. *Photograph property of the author*

Chapter Twenty-Eight

Marcel accompanied Martin and Joyce to their hotel, a comfortable accommodation near Place de la Republique. The square was still a chaotic collection of dirt and bricks and broken taxis from the bombing the previous Saturday. The statue of Marianne, surrounded by the same sandbag ramparts Martin had seen in Place Vendome, appeared to be unscathed. Her base was now also graced by bouquets of flowers and dozens of small tricolors. Since the first large shell landed in Quai de la Seine, bombs were falling randomly, seemingly out of nowhere. At first, Parisians looked-for high-flying zeppelins, or artillery hidden in the city itself. By the 23rd, however, French air reconnaissance had located the source of the projectiles, a giant German cannon located behind enemy lines near Coucy-le-Chateau-Auffrique in northern France. Because of the extreme distance and the huge trajectory, its operators had to factor the Coriolis Effect-the earth's rotation-into their calculations. The gun was notoriously inaccurate, but it expunged any war weary complacency among the Paris citizenry.

Martin was long accustomed to artillery by now. The possibility that a lone projectile might fall somewhere in the city didn't merit a second thought.

Martin knew Joyce and Marcel would be up and out early, so he made sure he was dressed and ready to say goodbye. He caught them as they waited for the car. Marcel continued to check his watch, while Joyce exhibited a distinct lack of enthusiasm for his upcoming introduction to the Paris literary scene.

"Trep, if I don't see you tonight or tomorrow before you leave, when you get back to the front, keep your head down. I hope to see you again soon."

Lieutenant Bouchard looked again at his watch and gave Martin a more military au revoir.

"Private Trep, it was an honor to accompany you. Enjoy the rest of your visit." And he finished with a perfect American salute.

Given the informality of the previous 24 hours, the gesture caught Martin by surprise. Still, it was a compliment coming from a commissioned officer, and he returned the salute with a smile.

As much as Martin enjoyed his guided tour, he was looking forward to an entire day where he could walk where he wanted, stop where he wanted, and enjoy the city at his leisure. His grasp of the language was rudimentary, but he felt confident walking around, thanks to a military city map left at the supply depot, plus the dozen or so books he had read about Paris and its history.

Paris is divided into twenty districts, or *arrondissements*. The districts spiral clockwise in an imperfect Fibonacci sequence, beginning with the neighborhood surrounding the Louvre and Place Vendome on the Right Bank. The Second Arrondissement is adjacent to the north, and then to the east, where Martin's hotel was located, is the Third. The Fifth and Sixth, and the Seventh, which includes the Eiffel Tower, are located across the Seine to the south, on the Left Bank. The Eighth is across the river again, and the districts wind around the city up to Twentieth, on the outskirts of Paris to the east. It was in the Eighteenth and Nineteenth where most of the Paris Gun shells landed the week before.

Very little that Marcel mentioned the previous day was new to Martin. As Marcel and Joyce learned to their surprise, he was well aware of the story of Heloise and Abelard, and in fact, he'd talked about them once with Pearl.

Leaving his hotel, Martin took a final look at the sandbag swaddled statue of Marianne, the revolutionaries' Lady Liberty, then walked east along Boulevard Saint-Martin and turned right at Boulevard de Sebastopol, until he crossed the Rue de Rivoli and came to the river. As much as Martin wanted to visit the Louvre, he was well aware of his time limits, and knew he could either spend the day in the museum or walking the city. He'd decided back at the supply depot that he would explore the city and save the museum for a future trip with Pearl.

Martin walked west along the river to Pont Neuf, and watched soldiers, families and workers crossing the bridge with no more in mind than getting to the other side. To Martin, however, the bridge embodied Paris history.

Pont Neuf was the oldest remaining bridge across the Seine. It connects the Right Bank, where Martin was standing, to *Ile de la Cite*, the small island in the middle of the river, and a southern span connects the island to the Left Bank. Looking upstream across the island to the east, was the original center of the city. Martin knew the bridge was a creation of Henri IV, and he knew it was Henri atop the equestrian statue in the middle of the span. Martin was well aware that Ben Franklin had written during the Revolutionary War that crossing the bridge helped him understand the Parisian character. Looking downstream, Martin recalled that the small spit of land just below the bridge once was a separate island-- *Ile aux Juifs*--where Jacques de Molay, the last grandmaster of the Knights Templar was burned at the stake in 1314.

Martin lingered on the bridge. He knew Pearl would laugh if he ever mentioned it to her, but here he felt he was truly connecting with French history. Still, he had but one day to see everything, and so he crossed the first span, and walked along the southern end of the island to the Cathedral of Notre Dame.

Martin always felt he was intruding when he visited a French church. He considered himself a good Christian and kept a bible in his personal belongings. He was not Catholic, however, and as he left the cathedral, he decided he would be more than just a tourist the next time he walked into a house of God. He figured God wouldn't refuse the prayers of a Lutheran who'd simply wandered into a different divine dwelling.

From Notre Dame, he crossed over to *Ile Saint-Louis*, the smaller island to the east. From there, he crossed again to the right bank, and stopped along Boulevard Henri IV for a bite to eat and a glass of wine. His next stop was the Pere Lachaise cemetery in the 20th. Martin felt refreshed after his lunch and decided to walk the narrow neighborhood streets toward the cemetery, rather than along the wide Haussmann boulevards. Martin stopped frequently, occasionally trying to converse with the locals, and eventually reached the cemetery named after the confessor to Louis XIV. Martin stopped first at the Communards' Wall, the site where the last revolutionaries were executed during the uprising of 1871. Martin then walked down the little hill to the crypt of Heloise and Abelard. The moment Marcel told him where they were interred, Martin resolved to visit. He'd brought along a pen and a sheet of paper from the hotel, and it took him but a moment to pen the note:

Pearl, Paris is everything I dreamed it to be.
When this war is over, we'll come here together,
and my happiness will be complete. I love you.

The structure resembles a tiny gothic church, open with arches on all four sides. He tossed the small, folded scrap of paper into the center of the crypt. He'd promised himself that he'd leave the paper and quickly depart, but his thoughts drifted back to Pearl. He wondered if she was enjoying a spring day in Cherokee, whether she'd be playing the piano that night, and most of all, whether she was thinking of him.

Leaving Pere Lachaise, Martin walked south along Avenue Philippe Auguste toward the Place de la Nation and another statue of Marianne, then to Picpus cemetery in the 12th. For the seasoned soldier, walking was no problem, and from the moment he realized he was going to Paris, Picpus was another priority. This stop, however, was not borne of romance. Every American soldier had heard by now of Colonel Charles Stanton's visit to the grave of the Marquis de Lafayette, the French general who fought alongside Washington in the Revolutionary War. Lafayette was buried next to his wife, and according to tradition, some of the soil covering the grave was brought back from Bunker Hill in 1825, when the Marquis visited America on the anniversary of that battle. On July 4, 1917, Colonel Stanton visited the tomb and planted an American flag, saying "Lafayette, we are here."

Martin found the grave immediately, and as he stood before the monument, a voice behind him said, "Bonjour, private. May I help you?"

Martin turned to see a man about his own age. He wore no uniform but carried an air of authority. As he stepped forward, Martin noticed the toes of the man's right foot stayed on the ground as he stepped, forcing him to lift his entire leg to move the recalcitrant appendage.

"Now you may tell Lafayette you are here as well. Welcome to Picpus Cemetery."

With a different tone, the comment might have seemed sarcastic, but it was simply matter of fact. Martin guessed the man was military.

"Thank you. I have a day in Paris, and …well… we've all heard about "Lafayette's tomb. Are you a caretaker here?"

The man laughed. "If only I had such responsibility. My job is to help young American soldiers find the famous tomb, and maybe, if they're so inclined, learn a little more about this place."

"Your English is excellent. May I ask…?"

"I studied in England before the war. Shortly after the mobilizations I was sent to translate for the English units on the Belgian border. On All Hallows Eve I was sent forward during the assault at Ypres, and I seem to have stumbled in front of a German machine gun. I took two in the arm, one in the ribs and my lung, and one in my right calf. That was the one the doctors told me was harmless. In a way they were right. It's rendered me harmless. I was Lieutenant Gagnon. Now I'm the Quasimodo of Picpus Cemetery, tour guide to the doughboys."

"I'm very sorry to hear about that, sir. But you're still translating, right? And you're showing your country to the

Americans, so the way I see it, you're still contributing. My name's Martin Treptow, and I'm happy to make your acquaintance. I don't have a lot of time, but you can tell me more about this cemetery."

Rene Gagnon had worked at Picpus since late 1917, and most of the American soldiers he met failed to show the proper respect for the place. This fellow was different. Something about the way he carried himself, and the way he smiled. Genuine. Rene figured the man made friends easily.

"I'm pleased to make your acquaintance, Private Treptow. I'm Rene' Gagnon. Once a lieutenant, now just the friend of Lafayette. If your time is short, let me show you a grave that tells you something about the French. Are you familiar with the Place de la Nation?"

"I walked through it this morning."

"The proximity is no coincidence. Follow me."

They proceeded through a gateway into a smaller enclosure. Martin lagged behind; figuring that if he walked slowly, his guide would feel less self-conscious about his labored gait. The walled area appeared to be –or maybe once was—a small garden. In the back stood a single, stark grey cross. Behind it, on the wall, were several plaques. They stopped before the crucifix and Rene' began his story,

"During the Reign of Terror, a guillotine was set up in the square, then called the *Place de Trone Renverz,* the Place of the Toppled Throne. This cemetery, only minutes away, became a convenient place to dump the decapitated bodies. On June 21, 1794, a small group of Carmelite nuns was arrested and sentenced to death. On July 17th, they were brought on two wooden carts to the square and killed one by one. It is said that when the first nun was taken to the scaffold, the mother superior led the sisters in chanting the Te Deum: *Benedicimus te, Domine Deus; te Dominum confitemur!* "We praise Thee, O God; we acknowledge Thee to be the Lord!" to which the sisters answered, *"Omnis terra venerator!"* "All the earth doth worship Thee!"

They walked around the cross, and Rene showed Martin the plaque that contained the names of the 16. By now Martin had witnessed killing on a grand scale, but it was still difficult to comprehend the senseless bloodshed of those long-ago summer months. He stood in silence for a few moments, then thanked Rene and bade his leave.

It was now mid-afternoon, and Martin still wanted to fulfill the promise to himself to visit a church and pray, and he also wanted a last stroll along the Seine. The city had been cloud covered since mid-morning, and Martin recalled Marcel telling him the day before that he should visit La Chapelle to see the windows, but only if the sun was out. He searched the city map for another church that he'd discovered in his readings and decided to make his final stop at St Gervais et St. Protais. The roundabout route would take him back to the river, and he could walk along the Right Bank almost to the church. He knew the edifice was constructed in the 16th century on the site of early Christian churches built a millennium earlier. He knew that saints Gervais and Protais were martyrs from northern Italy, and he recalled that because of the long period of construction, the French baroque facade contrasted with the gothic interior.

The church had been plundered and turned into the "Temple of Reason and Youth" during the French Revolution, before again becoming a house of God early in the 19th century. It was hard not to simply gape at the soaring arches along the side of the church and behind the altar, and even on a cloudy day, the stained-glass windows over the altar seemed to focus light straight down from heaven. But Martin came as a penitent, not a tourist. He found a seat and knelt in the Catholic style. He focused on the altar and began his prayer.

"Dear Lord, I hope it's okay for me to pray to you here. You know I'm not Catholic, but I promised I'd stop and pray, and my mother always told me you open your arms to everyone who will accept you.

"I've never felt very good about asking you for things. I know I could be a much better person, and I really don't deserve to be asking you for this and that. But I always say thanks, and I hope you know I'm trying. Anyway, most of what I want to ask you for ain't for me.

"Please watch over mother and father. My mother worries about me a lot, and my dad works real hard and I don't know if he's able to be there for my mother as much as he'd like. And Lord, please take care of my little brother. He has a good heart, and I love him dearly. Please keep him safe.

"I'm sorry for so many requests, Lord. I know you've done a good many things for me. Thank you for bringing me to Cherokee. Thank you for the talents you've given me. Thank you for Al, and all the good people I've met everywhere. And thank you for giving me Pearl. I know I should write to her more, and I'm sorry Lord. You know how much she means to me. And if it's your way that I don't return from this war, please let her be happy in life. Let her be successful and help her find a good man.

"Thank you for getting me through this war so far and thank you for helping me get over that scarlet fever. The doctors told me it could have damaged my insides, but I think I made it through. And thank you for protecting all the boys in the 168th. We're here fighting the good fight, and there is not a man in the trenches who doesn't believe you're watching over him.

"Finally, Lord, I have one last favor to ask. I know some of the boys would razz me, and some might get real mad if they heard me say this, but when this war is over, please help the Germans recover from this mess. President Wilson promised this will be the war to end all wars, and I sure hope he's right. I know those Huns believe what they're doing is right, and I think they believe in you, just like we do.

"Lord, I will do whatever you ask of me. Whatever your plans are for me, I know they're right and just.

"Thank you for listening Lord. Now I guess it's time for me to get back to the war."

Martin walked up the steps and entered quietly through the large doors opposite the altar. He walked along the side of the pews and stopped two thirds on the way to the front. He sat for a moment, and then renewed his conversation. He prayed for the taxi drivers who lost their lives in the Place de la Republique several days earlier in the bombing. He prayed that the souls of Heloise and Abelard were in heaven, and he prayed for the Carmelite nuns. He implored Jesus to watch over Joyce, and he prayed one more time for his family. Finally, in a soft voice, Martin prayed for himself.

"Lord, if it's not too much to ask, and I'm sorry for asking for so many things, but if you could find your way to keep me alive to the end of this war, I want to see my family, and I want to see Pearl. Thank you, God."

He stood up and made a Catholic sign of the cross and left the church.

From St Gervais, Martin walked northeast, again through the narrow streets, back to his hotel. He bathed, relaxed for a time, and then found a café where he enjoyed a quiet dinner and two small carafes of wine. Knowing it would be his last night in a comfortable bed for who knows how long, Martin slept in, bathed again, and walked north back to Gare de Nord. He waited only a short time for the next train, and by mid-afternoon on Wednesday, Martin was headed back to the 168th.

Two days later, on March 30th, 1918, one of the Paris Gun shells landed on the roof of St. Gervais et St. Protais, killing 90 parishioners during Good Friday services.

Chapter Twenty-Nine

In fact, it was not until Saturday, April 6th that Martin returned to his unit. The railway system grew more efficient with each passing month, but the movement of entire armies and tons of materiel took priority. Individual soldiers separated from their units had little choice but to bide their time and hope for an extra seat on a train heading in the right direction. By Friday the 5th, he'd gotten to Rambervillers, some 400 kilometers southeast of Paris and less than 30 kilometers from the 168th, entrenched at Neufmaisons to the northeast. Martin was excited to rejoin his unit, and frustrated when truck after truck was already filled or headed elsewhere. He had no choice but to spend another night waiting to return. His spirits were lifted a little when one of the YMCA workers allowed him to spend the night indoors on a davenport.

Martin woke the next morning to the guttural song of a drill sergeant. He looked out the window and saw at least 400 soldiers in formation heading through the town. Clean uniforms and wide eyes betrayed their recent arrival in France. They looked like the happy, dark-eyed young Italians Martin met in New York. But these fellows weren't smiling. Their formation was crisp, but even through the window Martin could sense an air of nervous anticipation.

As the unit passed the window, Martin was surprised to see their uniforms bore the insignia of the 42nd Division, 168th infantry. How could this be? He pulled on his pants, not bothering with shirt or shoes, and ran outside. He stopped a young lieutenant watching the formation pass. Martin saluted, and noticed the officer shared the insignia. "Sir. Private Martin Treptow."

"At ease, Private. What can I do for you?"

"Sir, well I was wondering about this unit. You see, I'm also with the 168th and…"

"Why are you here then?"

"I was in a hospital, sir, and I've been trying to get back to the unit."

"These men are replacements, Private. They'll be shipping out to Neufmaisons at 1400. There'll be room for you Private, and you best find your uniform and be on one of the trucks."

"Yes, sir!"

The convoy left at precisely 1400 hours, and proceeded north to Baccarat, then headed east. It was dark when the trucks rolled in to Neufmaisons. No sooner had he stepped out of the back when he heard "Trep, you scarlet fever son of a bitch!" It was his friend and bunkmate, Bill Klema.

The next voice he heard was Lieutenant John Currie of the Third Battalion. "Welcome back, Private barber! We got a battalion of sheep dogs waiting for you. Grab a night's sleep, then sharpen your scissors and report to me tomorrow."

Martin was back at the front.

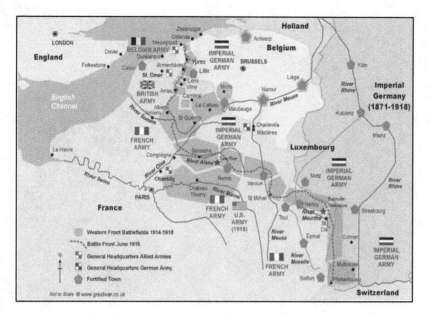

Map of Western Front 1914-18. *Reprinted with permission of Greatwar.co.uk*

Chapter Thirty

It was several days before Martin found time to write letters home. He also had to deal with another matter. Shortly after he rejoined his unit, headquarters received a message from the supply depot at Nogent-sur-Marne. A certain Private Treptow had distinguished himself during his brief stay, and the supply sergeant had requested his transfer. This would virtually ensure he'd spend the war away from the front, but Martin would have none of it. After making his intention clear to Lieutenant Currie and Sergeant McManus, he returned to his cot and penned a letter home:

> *Back home again with my company. You'd think I was a lieutenant or a company commander the way I start this letter-"my company"! Nothing to it! I'm still a buck private in the rear rank but I'm holding my own and the Germans haven't got me yet. But, believe me, the Ginks have some mighty hot shells, but Uncle Sam's are a bit hotter. It can't help but back up and take water... Lost a couple of men, but Uncle Sam has thousands to take the places of the poor boys who have left us. I sure did hate to see the boys get killed, Al, but we can't all come home...*

> *Just got back from the hospital but will be with the boys next time they go if I'm not transferred. Heard this afternoon that I am transferred, but the first sergeant told me at mess that they were going to try and keep me and a couple of the other boys. Hope they do-have been*

transferred enough. Great old war, Al; better than none at all.

There we go-just heard a shell burst. Haven't time to think about it-must get this letter out today. Perhaps there won't be a tomorrow. Funny country over here. Sometimes they don't have a tomorrow, but always a yesterday.

I'm going to try and send Pearl a picture of a hole that a hand grenade made when it went off. Ask her to let you see it. At this very hole two Germans met their Waterloo some time ago. How is Cherokee and everybody? Got a fine little Cherokee over here, but it's all shot to hell. No American Theatre here, but a fine American army.

...

Passed your letters to all the boys. They all appreciated them as much as I did. Every time I get a letter from you all, the boys want to see it. Regards to all.

M.A. Treptow

The following day, Martin he was happy to learn he'd be staying with the 168th. The Third Battalion was still off the line, and Martin celebrated the non-transfer by sharing some of his recent adventures:

Dear Al:

Don't know what to do with myself this morning so guess I will spend a bit of my time in writing you a letter. I'm going to try you just once more. I've written you several times but always fail to get an answer to my letters.

This is a great old world, Al. Just wish I could sit down in the old shop and tell you people of our experiences and things we have seen. Many a time while at home I remember of my mother reading the bible to us and showing us pictures, myself never dreaming of seeing those different places. But at present I have seen a number of places here that are pictured in the Bible. Went through a place here some time ago which was built in 1066 by the Normans. Also saw a well built by the Normans a thousand years ago. Have seen houses here that were built in the year 1320. Doesn't seem possible, but nevertheless, it is still standing with a family living in it. One thing great over here-you get to mingle with people of every nation in the entire world. Got to talking with a Scotch Highlander here this winter. He was telling me of different things he had seen and done while going over the top.

The reason I did not write before is on account of being in a hospital for several weeks.

M. A. Treptow

Chapter Thirty-One

Mademoiselle from Armentieres Parlez-vous

Mademoiselle from Armentieres Parlez-vous

You didn't have to know her long

To know the reason men go wrong

Hinky-dinky Parlez-vous

(Mademoiselle from Armentieres)

Traditional

Martin was being typically diplomatic in describing the Scottish Highlander. The man had come with the trucks to Neufmaissons and just stayed on. He wasn't connected to any American or French units, and the English were not in the Lorraine sector. He was as wide as he was tall and wore his Scottish Kilt rather than the English uniform, explaining, "I need to air out me arse!" The man was hard to dislike--he had a story for every occasion and treated the men to more verses of *Mademoiselle from Armentieres* than they'd ever heard before.

Still, the Scotsman was not without his flaws. He fancied himself a lady's man, a belief to which he was a congregation of one. His crude flirtations annoyed the nurses and YMCA workers, and his leers frightened the village girls. He also exhibited his prejudices. By this stage of the war, American Negro units had seen extensive combat. Thousands of

Moroccans had died alongside their French comrades at Verdun, and the Anamese, while generally noncombatants, were invaluable ambulance and supply drivers. Even the Alabamans in the 167th understood that if the Negroes weren't there supporting them, they'd be unloading supplies and burying their dead themselves. Once a man spent a month at the front, he saw little value in denigrating a fellow soldier because of the color of his skin.

The Scotsman respected the white Americans, and for the most part, countenanced the French, but he had no good words for American Negroes or French colonials. His prejudices were subtle, but constantly expressed; men he considered less than his equals were typically the butt of some bad joke.

The man eventually tested even the famous hospitality of the Iowans. No one confronted him, however, partially because of his enormous build, but also--Martin figured--sometimes it's hard to argue with a man who's not arguing with you. Nevertheless, the men of Company M began looking for a way to deliver a comeuppance.

The Third Battalion was still off the line, and Martin, barbering to the entire 168th, was billeted in an abandoned house. Each day was warmer than the last, and cherry blossoms temporarily masked the smells of war. Martin decided it would be a good day to be outside, so he took three chairs, his shaving kit and scissors, and a large sheet liberated from one of the rooms and moved his business into the sun. He'd finished five or six of the Company K men when the Highlander came down the street.

"Twenty francs says yeh canna shave me close!"

"I'll take that bet," said Martin. "Let me finish this guy, and I'll do you next." Martin toweled off an Iowa private, and the hefty Scotsman plopped into the chair.

The large man leaned back and rubbed his bearded, pock-marked face. "You'll never get these cheeks shaved clean, laddie. There're too many crags for yeh."

Martin wrapped the sheet around the man's neck, swished the brush, and applied an even film of shaving cream. "Now," he told the man, "take this little ball and put it in your mouth, then push it against your right cheek."

The man did as he was told, and Martin's straight razor took every bit of hair from the taut skin.

"You've gotten the better of me, boy. If you can match the other side, this will be the best shave I've had here in Hades." He shifted the orb to the other cheek. "Say, what would happen if I'd swallow this little ball?"

"No problem at all," Martin replied. "I was shaving a Negro the other day, and he swallowed that same ball. Brought it back just this morning."

They didn't see the Highlander after that day, and Martin never collected on the bet. A wag remarked that if the French artillery could shoot as far as the Scotsman spit that little ball, they'd have no need for the Americans.

Chapter Thirty-Two

Late April 1918. Lorraine sector

They were coming back down to Badonvillar and met supply wagons rumbling up to the trenches. The company stood down while the wagons passed, and Martin decided to walk up the hill to a small glove of trees. They were fruit of some sort, festooned with white spring blossoms. It was the scents, though, not the colors that captured his attention.

Martin walked among the trees and tried to forget the putrid stench of war. The blossoms were wonderfully pungent, and for a moment Martin was back at the farm on a warm spring day enjoying the scent of lilacs flowering by the porch.

The moment passed too soon. Try as he might, he couldn't even briefly escape the stink of war. Even in the trees, he smelled the horses passing with supply wagons, and he smelled his wool uniform that had entertained rain and sweat and mud over the past fortnight. And he looked at a comrade's dried blood on his sleeve and he thought of the worst stink of all -the stench of death. Growing up on the farm, Martin had seen death and smelled it. Mice and cats and cows and horses. If the big animals weren't buried or hauled away, the mephitis permeated everything for a short time. It never lasted long, and Martin came to look upon that smell as the animal's last communication with the sentient world.

A week ago, Martin's patrol found the forward German trench unoccupied, and ventured ahead toward the enemy's main lines. They came upon the putrefied bodies of a German officer and his horse, both half-eaten by wolves. Apparently, the officer had felt confident enough to mount up between the trenches. His gamble had failed.

The stink of those rotting corpses provided no hint of closure, but only portended more death to come. Ten minutes among fruit blossoms couldn't erase the memory of that awful smell.

Chapter Thirty-Three

The spring German offensives at the Somme and to the north didn't materialize in the Lorraine, and the 168th's duties were confined to rotating in and out of the trenches, more drilling, and patrolling no man's land. Each battalion formed scouting patrols from volunteers. Commanding the Third Battalion scouts were Lieutenants Bradley, Jones, and Currie. The Third Battalion also had a designated Chief Scout Officer, Lieutenant Walter Schaefer of Company G. Lieutenant Schaefer was an Iowa boy, and a college football star. He reminded Martin of Gus: strong, smart, and fearless but not foolhardy. He didn't need to yell or jump up and down to get the men to follow him. Men sensed his confidence immediately, and he made them confident as well. Scout volunteers always considered their endeavor a little safer when they learned the lieutenant would be leading.

The enlisted men were not required to volunteer for scout duty, but eventually most of the men served a patrol or two. Some were guys who thrived on the danger - the kind who jumped off the Cobban Bridge back home and never checked to see how deep the water was running. There also were guys who'd been in the trenches too often and got crazy when things got quiet. Those fellas volunteered all the time, and Martin wondered what would become of them when they got back home, if they got back home. Most of the volunteers, however, were men who just figured everyone needed to step up and serve a turn. Martin was one of those guys.

By now, the 168th was familiar with the enemy's habits. The forward trenches hadn't shifted for some time, and the only question was whether they were currently occupied. This was one of the purposes of the scouts' patrol. On Saturday, April 20th, the Third Battalion had rotated out of the trenches, and Lieutenant Currie sought volunteers from M Company for a scouting party. The men had recently heard that Baron von Richthofen had shot down his 80th allied plane. The news made the men more eager to seek a measure of retribution, and with the war in the trenches at a standstill, the only way to meet the enemy was to go on patrol. Martin volunteered, figuring it was just about his turn, and with some reluctance, Bill joined him. At 21:30, led by Lieutenant Bradley, a team from K and M Companies left the allied lines and headed into no man's land. The patrol formed a double arrowhead formation past the Americans' forward trenches, toward a ruined farm just in front of what they believed were the German lines.

The farm sat atop a small hill, and no sooner had the patrol started up the slope when a flare shot up ahead of them. Everyone took cover, but to their relief, the illumination was not followed by gunfire or artillery. The K Company detachment lead by Sergeant McHugh headed off to the right, toward the source of the flares, hoping to draw fire and locate the Germans' exact position and determine their strength. However, no sooner had the detachment moved away, when an entire platoon of Germans was detected moving on the left of the M Company scouts. They made no effort to hide themselves. Except for the fact that they were wearing helmets and carrying rifles, they could have been out for a walk in the park. Lieutenant Bradley, recognizing immediately that his small patrol was outnumbered, gave an immediate order: "Give 'em everything you got!" The small patrol opened up with every weapon at their disposal, and to their relief, the German platoon retreated in absolute double-quick toward its own lines. At that point, the men from Company K returned, and Lieutenant Bradley elected not to push his luck.

The patrol took note of the German killed and wounded and retreated back to the Americans' forward trench.

Some days later, the Third Battalion rotated back into the trenches. Each battalion served in the trenches for eight days, then rotated off the line, then to reserve, then back to the front. Lieutenant Bradley asked for another group of volunteers, to allow the new rotation to familiarize itself with the current position of the enemy and the occupation of its trenches. Martin again volunteered, and this time, Lieutenant Bradley was accompanied by two other lieutenants and a rifle team to protect their flank. Martin was pleased to see that one of the additional officers was Lieutenant Schaefer.

Their goal on this night was forward reconnaissance, all the way to the leading German trench. It was overcast and rainy, and the starless night allowed the patrol to cut the German wire and move forward without detection. They reached the forward German trench, called Mecklenburg, and found it unoccupied. Exiting the other side, they moved forward unchallenged. Just then, however, someone coughed, and immediately flares went up. The men took cover and made no sound, waiting to see if flares would be followed by gunfire. Hearing nothing, Lieutenant Shaefer waived the men forward.

No sooner had they'd taken five steps, however, when the German line opened up. Flares turned night into day, and the patrol had nowhere to hide. The men scattered into shell holes and retreated from crater to crater. The patrol regrouped into the Germans' trench, then realized that Lieutenants Mackay and Schaefer were not with them. Fortunately, the Germans didn't pursue, and Lieutenant Bradley directed the men to wait for the two officers. Eventually Lieutenant Mackey dived into the trench and reported that Lieutenant Schaefer was seriously wounded and could not be brought back to the lines. The next morning, another patrol sent to locate Lieutenant Schaefer found only his helmet. A week later, they learned from a German prisoner that Wally Schaefer, the pride of Ottumwa, who'd played fullback for Amos Alonzo Stagg at the University of Chicago, was retrieved by German medical officers, but died the next day and was buried near Cirey-sur-Vezouse several miles to the north.

Chapter Thirty-Four

Neufmaisons

"Are you looking for the Blue Line?"

"I'm sorry?"

"The Blue Line. You were looking in the distance. If you're looking for it, you're on the wrong side of the mountains."

The woman was maybe 60. Martin could tell by her coat she wasn't a nurse, or with the YMCA. Her English was excellent; he thought British perhaps.

"I'm sorry; I don't know what the Blue Line is."

"You Americans. We're west of the Vosges Mountains. There is a legend that on a foggy evening, the round mountain tops glow a blueish haze. But we're really too close to the mountains to see it. It's better to watch the sunset looking west from the Alsace. Perhaps one day after the war is over you can visit, if the Boche haven't destroyed everything. Some of the towns, like Riquewihr and Colmar haven't changed much in 500 years. You would find them very beautiful."

"I love history, and they sound wonderful. I'm sorry that I know so little of your country. I know about Charlemagne and Joan of Arc and Napoleon, and I'd love to learn more, but the war keeps interfering with my studies. I'm sorry; I didn't catch your name."

She laughed. "Do all Americans apologize so often? My name is Marie. Do you have a name-and a cigarette?"

Martin pulled the silver case from his breast pocket. He half expected the woman to decline his proffer, but she quickly took out a cigarette, tamped the end, and lit up.

"My name is Martin. They call me Trep. May I ask you something?"

"My English?"

"You speak very good English, but you don't sound American, and you don't sound quite British."

"My family's estate is-was-just outside Badonviller. My parents sent me to England at the outset of the last war. I grew up north of London, and when I was a teenager, I made the mistake of falling in love. We divorced in 1910, and I returned home just in time to salvage our family's holdings. I managed to stay out of the way when the bombs started falling. Then the French authorities realized the value of an old woman who could speak English and French and move across the lines without attracting attention. The Germans never guess that I am a "*francs-tireurs*"-a partisan."

"You're a spy?"

"That sounds very romantic and exciting, Trep. But I'm just an old woman who goes about her business, makes observations, and sometimes shares them. And these days my job is to explain to my countrymen what exactly you Americans are trying to say when they hear "bone sawyer", or "mercy boo-coop.""

Martin smiled sheepishly. "I'm glad you speak English. So, tell me more about Alsace and Lorraine."

"Where would you like me to start, Private Trep? The Blue Line is now the front. The lands to the east were a spoil of 1870, but the Alsace will always be French to the Rhine. To a Frenchman, a good border is crossed easily, to foster commerce and social intercourse. To us, the Rhine is a perfect border. The Germans like a border they can defend. The Vosges Mountains are their ideal border. And so, poor little Alsace, between the mountains and the river, has been fought over for centuries. Fifty years of occupation have brought many Germans to the Lorraine as well, so take heed private, some of these villagers may not be your friends".

"I'll be careful. Tell me more about the Lorraine. North of Badonviller- in the fields to the east-there are yellow flowers. What are they?"

"*Les Jouquilles*. Wild daffodils."

"And the trees with the white flowers?"

"*Les mirombelliers*. The Mirabelles. They're just beginning to bloom. The blossoms are beautiful, and perhaps you'll be here to taste the fruit. The plums are unlike any other.

"Private Trep, you're very observant. I'm impressed. Now you say you know of Jeanne d'Arc?

"To the west, where the Lorraine becomes the Champagne is the village of Domremy-la-Pucelle. She was born there, and her home still stands.

"You are a man of God, Private Trep?"

"War seems to make a fellow religious. I was raised a Lutheran."

"There are many Lutherans here. Perhaps one day you'll visit the beautiful Lutheran church in Strasbourg. What do you do when you are not in the trenches, private? Do you enjoy wine, perhaps?"

"I've learned to enjoy your vin rouge over the last few months."

"You need to try our vin blanc. Our white wine is like no other. It's called Riesling, and once you drink it, all other wines will be found wanting. Do you enjoy a good cheese, private?"

"I grew up on a farm, ma'am. I've been eating cheese all my life."

"So, you are a connoisseur? Surely then you've heard of Munster."

"I have not."

"You must try it. And I'm sure you'll tell me you know all about cows as well."

"I've milked my share."

"Our cows here are special. They were bred over centuries by the monks. Our butter and our cheeses are the best in France. Have you ever had a *quiche Lorraine*?"

"A what?"

"It's a ham, egg, and cheese tart. Someday when this war is over, and we can again fatten the hogs and find grain for the chickens, perhaps you'll be able to enjoy this special dish. I make mine with potatoes. Someday I'll be able to grow them again."

"There must be ground somewhere to grow crops?"

"Furrowed with bombs? Fertilized with mustard gas? I think not. After the bombings of 1914, we started a little garden in the park off Rue Gabbard by Eglise San Martin."

"The bombed dome?"

"Yes. But now your American friends play base ball there when the guns are quiet."

"Do you still have spuds from last year?"

"I do, and I'm sure others do as well. But where would we plant?"

"Marie, I have an idea."

Chapter Thirty-Five

Sunday April 28, 1918

"Get up, Bill! I've got a job for you."

"Trep, my job is to get reacquainted with my cot. It missed me dearly when we were in the trenches, and now that the battalion's rotated out this is what I am going to do as long as the army will allow me."

"Bill, get your butt outta bed. We're going to help the French."

"I'm helping the French right now. I'm saving up my energy to push the Huns across the Rhine. Isn't that enough?"

"Bill, we're going to help the locals. Do you know how to plant potatoes?"

"Of course, I do. And I also know how to plant my butt in this cot."

"Bill, get up. It's a beautiful spring day."

Bill knew he was licked. Never mind that he outranked him. Trep just wasn't the kind of guy you could say no to. He'd known him since the earliest 168th encampment at the Iowa fairgrounds. He'd been his bunkmate at Camp Mills, on the R.M.S. *Celtic* and here in Neufmaisons. Trep never had cross words for anyone, and he was always doing things that made the guys appreciate him. There were fellows who did that just to kiss the ass of the officers. Trep did things because they were the right things to do. The guy was liked by every man in the company, and Bill guessed, maybe everyone in the 168th infantry whose hair Trep had ever cut. If a new replacement wasn't his friend, it just meant they'd never met. Guy like that asks you for a favor, it's harder than hell to say no.

Bill could only sigh. "Alright, Trep. What exactly are we gonna do?"

"I met a French woman who lives outside of Badonviller. She said everyone's gardens are now bomb craters, trenches and barbed wire, and she's afraid the people will have a rough time of it in the fall. They have seed potatoes from last year, and there's a two-acre plot by the Eglise San Martin that's not used for anything but base ball."

"So, let me get this straight, Trep. You and I are going to convince the army to give up a two-acre field, and then you and I are going to plant two acres of potatoes. Do I have that right?"

"Of course not. I'm going to talk to Lieutenant Currie, who is going to talk to the Major, who's going to give us permission to plant that field. Then you and I are going to talk to the rest of M Company, and whoever else is rotating off the line, and we're going to plant these folks some potatoes."

Lieutenant Currie had reservations.

"Private Treptow, I can't guarantee you that regiment ain't going to need that space, and I can't promise what the Major is going to say. You know the scuttlebutt. It's possible we won't even be here for long. Now that Foch has taken over the AEF, this unit could be going God knows where. What I'm hearing is that there will be another offensive to the southeast of Reims, and if that happens, we'll be plugged into that hole. M Company may not be here to finish that planting, and we certainly won't be around to harvest."

"Sir, the locals can harvest. But if we can just get started and the war moves elsewhere, they can finish the planting. You know there are lots of locals who aren't so sure the side that's here right now is the right side. A little thing like this might help convince 'em."

"I imagine you want me to ask the Major. I'll tell you what. You ask him yourself. I don't think this idea of yours will go anywhere. But be my guest."

The Major turned out to be a much easier sell. Shortly after Martin returned to his unit, he'd given the Major what he said was the best haircut he'd gotten since he left home. And so, Martin, Bill, and about a third of M Company became farmers for a day. At first the New York replacements had some reservations. But Martin remembered what Gus taught him back on the Cameron railroad. He bet one of the Long Island sergeants that Iowa boys could work the land twice as fast as his city fellas. It cost Martin a platoon of free haircuts, but those two acres were planted in record time.

Members of the 168th Infantry planting potatoes near Eglise San Martin, Badonvillars, France, Spring 1918. *Photograph property of the author.*

Chapter Thirty-Six

By late 1917, the German High Command concluded that a war of attrition couldn't be won. Their citizenry was growing increasingly restive, and the lines in the west had not changed appreciably since 1916. The generals also understood, though, that circumstances had bequeathed them a temporary advantage. The collapse of Czarist Russia allowed several divisions to be moved away from the Eastern Front, and the March 1918 Treaty of Brest-Litovsk ended the war against Russia completely. The United States had declared war in April 1917, but mobilization was proceeding slowly, and the generals questioned whether the American Expeditionary Force would ever be a factor.

In mid-November 1917, General Erich Ludendorff proposed a major spring offensive, consisting of a series of large frontal attacks, beginning near Saint Quentin on the Somme, some 120 kilometers north and east of Paris. The goal was to separate the English and French armies and force the Allies to sue for peace.

The operation, named after St. Michael, Germany's patron saint, began on March 21st. In the first five hours of the attack, the Germans fired over 3,000 artillery shells per minute along a 60-mile front. By the end of the day, the British had suffered over 18,000 casualties. Another 21,000 were taken prisoner. The resulting German advance across the Somme was the largest breakthrough on the Western Front since 1914. It allowed the giant Paris Guns to be moved within striking distance of that city, where two of the 183 shells landed in the Place de la Republique, and on the roof of St. Gervais et St. Protais. On March 24th, Kaiser Wilhelm II declared a national holiday, and the war-weary German people hoped the conflict would soon be over.

What the generals did not anticipate was the amount of manpower sacrificed to achieve their gains. German casualties numbered almost 40,000, and the logistical strain of dealing with the high number of wounded, thousands of prisoners, and stretched supply lines caused the offensive to bog down.

The second wave of the attack, named Georgette, was launched on April 9th, near Ypres, close to the French-Belgian border. The Germans retook the Passchendaele Ridge, where the British had sacrificed so many the previous year. Like Michael, it resulted in a German victory, but was similarly achieved at great cost. In two months, the Germans had suffered almost a quarter of a million casualties, and the temporary advantage gained by America's slow mobilization was about to be lost. By the end of March, 250,000 Americans were in France, and the number increased by 10,000 per day.

In late May, the Germans launched another wave, named Blucher-Yorck, between Soissons and Reims, east of Paris. Again, the offensive was an initial success, and due to its proximity to Paris-less than 50 miles from the western edge of the salient-the offensive was cause for great alarm in the allied camp. The assault was coupled with waves of gas attacks in the Lorraine, where the 168th was stationed.

The Blucher-Yorck bulge stretched from Soissons south to Chateau-Thierry, and northeast to Reims. It was in this sector that the American Expeditionary Force, including the Rainbow Division, would see their first large scale fighting. When the Germans advanced to the Marne, the U.S. Third Infantry was rushed to Chateau-Thierry, and together with French units, stopped the German advance. It was here that Colonel Ulysses

Grant McAlexander, and later his entire 38th Infantry Regiment, earned the title "Rock of the Marne."

In early June, the Germans focused their attack on the western edge, near Belleau Wood. French forces and U.S. Marines blunted the attack, and on the morning of June 6th, units of the Fifth and Sixth Marine Divisions counterattacked through open wheat fields and a former game preserve. The Marines suffered almost 10,000 casualties during the initial assaults and didn't secure the forest and town for another three weeks. The battle was among the bloodiest fought by Americans during the entire war, and it earned "Belleau Wood" a place in the pantheon of United States Marine lore.

General Ludendorff had decided in July to move his First, Third, and Seventh armies east of Reims to make a break toward Paris, calling the plan "Friedensturm", the Peace Offensive. Allied victories at Chateau-Thierry and Belleau Wood blunted and ultimately helped close the Blucher-Yorck salient. French and American armies then launched a counter-offensive, resulting in what became, for the Germans, a three-and-a-half-month retreat. Ludendorff's final gamble had not paid off, and only much later would he come to appreciate the irony of the title.

Soldiers of the 168th heading north from Neufmaisons, France,
Spring 1918. *Photograph property of the author.*

Chapter Thirty-Seven

Beat your plowshares into swords, and your
pruning hooks into spears. Let the
weak say I am strong.

Joel 3:10

News of the St. Michael offensive reached the 168th, but to everyone's relief, the Lorraine sector remained quiet. The Americans stepped up their patrols in late April and May, and the Germans displayed no inclination to make this eastern portion of their lines part of the larger operation. This was soon to change.

In the final days of April, the Rainbow Division's general staff elected to make a push through the German lines. The artillery bombardment began on May 1st, and on the 3rd, units of the 166th went over the top. The ultimate result was a gain of three lines of trenches and a step up of artillery from both sides that lasted throughout the month. In mid-May, when M Company and the Third Battalion occupied the forward trench, French heavy artillery miscalculated the distance and rained shells on the American lines. A half-dozen of Martin's comrades were killed before the error could be corrected.

The Third Battalion rotated off the front on the 17th, and the men looked forward to sixteen days in reserve or behind the lines. At 1:00 a.m. on the 27th, however, all three battalions of the 168th came under a sudden, large-scale gas attack.

The use of gas had evolved significantly since Ypres. At first, the armies employed chlorine. Exposure caused coughing, vomiting and eye irritation. Fully inhaled, the water-soluble gas formed hydrochloric acid in the lungs. Soldiers soon learned to recognize the greenish haze, and the unique popping sounds of the gas projectiles. Each division headquarters had a gas chamber for practice attacks, and the men were drilled and re-drilled in the use of their masks. The late May attack was timed to afford little opportunity to prepare, however. Men off the trenches were asleep, and most had no time to put on their masks. There also was no pale green cloud. This time the Germans used phosgene, colorless and with less odor than chlorine, but significantly more toxic. Its initial effects mimicked chlorine, but over the next day or two, fluid would build up in the lungs, frequently causing death. Phosgene would kill 80,000 combatants by war's end.

The gas attack was followed immediately by an artillery assault, then more gas shells were dropped on Pexonne and Badonviller. Soon a steady stream of ambulances transferred casualties to Baccarat, some 15 kilometers to the west, where the regiment's oxygen treatment center was located.

The gas dissipated for the most part during the following days but lingered in the low areas. Due to the high number of casualties in the front lines, several companies of the Second Battalion returned to the trenches on May 30th. As Company M marched forward to its reserve position, Martin saw before him a tableau of death. Plants and grasses were scarred yellow, with cats and rats frozen in rigor mortis and bloating. Martin recalled a late October killing frost on the farm. Green leaves immediately browned and shriveled, and a neighbor's cow died frozen in a pond. The grim spectacle before him now, however, came with no promise of a future spring.

As soon as the Third Battalion was situated in its reserve position, Martin tried to catch up on his letter writing. The gas attacks had taken a grim toll, and Martin and the men of Cherokee all had lost friends and comrades. On the 31st, he wrote a letter to Al, telling him:

> *Couldn't get out to the graves of our men yesterday, so Klema and I went out today and put flowers on them. The graves are very pretty and green. We have a large flag on Corporal Behmer's grave.*

Having paid tribute to the fallen, Martin tried his best to impart a cheerier tone:

> *The boys were all lined up waiting for supper and I'm not very hungry tonight-won't go down to supper. The fellow who is rooming with me has gone downtown after a half dozen eggs and some jam and we are going to have lunch here in our room tonight. We have two rooms upstairs-use one for a barber shop and the other for a living room. Broke my clippers today-don't know what I'll do for clippers now.*
> *...*
> *Band concert to play, Al; I'm going down to take it in. First time I've heard music in a month. Reminds me of a band concert in Cherokee.*

M. A. Treptow

French girls place flowers on the graves of soldiers from the 168th killed in the May 1918 gas attacks. Baccarat, France, May 31,1918. Martin's letter, above, indicates that Bill Klema and he visited the graves the same day. *Photograph property of the author.*

Chapter Thirty-Eight

Regimental command didn't realize it at the time, but the gas attacks and subsequent bombardment were intended to keep the Rainbow Division occupied in the Baccarat sector in the east, while Blucher-Yorck got underway in the west. The Third Battalion returned to the front lines on June 7th. On the 15th, expecting to be relieved, they were ordered to stay put for a few more days until the entire division could be transferred. Rumors were that the 168th would be rotated off the front for a much-needed rest. Since arriving in the sector, the First Battalion had suffered 240 casualties, the Second, owing to the good fortune of having rotated into the trenches during quiet periods, had lost only 37, and the Third 140. On June 18th the 168th moved out of the sector and by the 20th was billeted in Baccarat. The respite didn't last long; from there the unit marched almost continually for the next ten days, to the Champagne and the valley of the Marne.

On July 4th, the 168th reached Nantwet, 30 kilometers east and south of Reims. That night, in anticipation of the German attack, the First and Third battalions moved into positions near the front. They spent the next week under artillery fire, preparing for what their commanders believed was an imminent offensive. The Rainbow Division at this time was attached to the French Fourth Army, commanded by General Henri Gouraud, the one-armed hero of Gallipoli. On July 7th, believing the attack was immediately forthcoming; General Gouraud issued his famous order:

We may be attacked at any moment. You all know that a defensive battle was never engaged under more favorable conditions. We are awake and on our guard. We are powerfully reinforced with infantry and artillery.

You will fight on a terrain which you have transformed by your labor and perseverance into a redoubtable fortress-an invincible fortress if all its entrances are well guarded.

The bombardment will be terrible; you will face it without weakness; the assault will be fierce in clouds of smoke, dust, and gas; but your position and your armament are formidable. In your breasts beat the brave and strong hearts of free men.

None shall glance to the rear; none shall yield a step. Each shall have but one thought; to kill, to kill many, until they've had enough.

Therefore, your General says to you: "You will break this assault, and it will be a happy day."

General Gouraud's order was read to the men in the late afternoon. After dinner, Martin sat down and wrote a short note to his friends in Cherokee:

I'm going beat you to it and write first. I've been waiting for the word to go home. I suppose some Hun will give me a good beating one of these days. I'll be asleep when he does. I'm one of the brave boys you read about, but it's all in my own writing.

Best wishes. M. A. Treptow

Over the next week reconnaissance and prisoner information confirmed that an offensive would soon begin. However, Bastille Day saw no enemy action, and Martin and the rest of the M Company spent the afternoon of the 14th teaching their French counterparts American football. Martin asked to play quarterback, but Private Bob Reed, a friend from Red Oak, reminded everyone that he was gassed back in the Lorraine and had no wind. So Bob played quarterback. Martin then asked to play halfback, but Louie Weiss, a young man from Woodbine, argued that Martin had a longer reach, and was a better fit at the end position. Reed had a good arm, and Martin caught his share of passes. Nursing a beer after the game, Martin thought about Gus. He figured if they met again, he'd thank him for making the forward pass so popular.

That evening, Martin penned a letter to Mr. and Mrs. Swenson, with whom he'd boarded during his days in Cherokee: His letter read in part:

A year at the old game today and no furlough in sight. Don't care a great deal about one as we couldn't get much of a chance to spend it anyway. All I ask is to give me a furlough after this war. Sometimes it seems it won't be long and then again it doesn't look as bright, but we all know it can't last a great deal longer

...

Bob Spurlock

Just a year ago today I held up my hand and said I'd do it.
Am not one bit sorry of it.

Chapter Thirty-Nine

Anticipating the assault, French and AEF artillery opened up just before midnight on the 14th. Twenty minutes later the enemy responded, and over the next eleven hours the 168th endured the most furious, sustained artillery assault of their entire war. At daybreak, the Third Battalion was ordered to a position immediately behind the allied trenches. The shelling was now in its seventh hour. The men in the column could scarcely hear each other speak and couldn't always make out the sound of shells about to drop in their midst. The constant threat prevented any semblance of formation; the men would move 20 steps forward, sometimes 100, before the whine of incoming would have them diving for the nearest bomb crater.

Privates Reed and Weiss were some 70 feet ahead of Martin as the company moved forward. Suddenly an incoming projectile landed just behind the two privates. New replacements stared wide eyed, and one fell to his knees and retched. On the road in front of them were Weiss' boots, with his feet and parts of his lower legs still in them. His upper torso was blown forward into the ditch, and his head, now grotesquely propped by a single arm, faced the company. His eyes were still open. He'd died before his nervous system had a chance to register any shock. Martin and the more experienced members of his platoon stepped around Weiss' boots and attended to Reed, who was alive, but barely. A foot was blown away, and his left arm remained connected only by a scrap of skin. Blood gushed from a hole in his right leg, and one of the men created a barbed wire and stick tourniquet to stanch the flow. Reed was strangely calm, and he recognized Martin. "Trep, next time I'll throw more balls your way. You have good hands."

Martin could find no words, and simply held Reed's head up as they placed him on the stretcher to head back to the dressing station. Martin learned later that he lived just long enough to start a final cigarette and make his peace with God before Chaplin Robb.

The bombardment continued on and off for the next two days, but by late afternoon of the 15th, the men knew the anticipated attack was not focused on their sector. French and AEF units repulsed the enemy to the north, near Soissons, and late in the evening of the 18th, the 168th received orders to withdraw some ten kilometers south of Suippes, southeast of Reims. They moved quickly, to get beyond the range of spotter planes and artillery fire before daybreak. On the 19th, the 168th arrived at Camp de la Noblette near Chalons, where Attila the Hun met defeat in 451A.D. Martin opened his journal and made a short entry:

July 1918, arrived at French Rest Camp at
9:30a.m. Expect to stay and rest for two days.

The camp featured real barracks, a nearby stream for bathing and de-lousing, and a fully stocked-and very busy-mess. On the 20th, junior officers were granted leave to visit Chalons-sur-Marne. The truck had additional room, and the enlisted men held a lottery. Martin was content to have an entire day to sleep, eat hot meals, and write letters. Shortly after lunch, he sat on the edge of his cot and began a letter to Pearl.

Dear Ms. Van de Steeg:

I know it's been too long since I last wrote, but we've been in the thick of things for two weeks. I'm not in the Lorraine anymore. The 168th was asked to stop a Hun assault in the Champagne, which is close to Reims if you want to find it on a map.

Pearl--and I know I never use your first name when I write -- a few days ago I saw two friends I played football with the day before get blown up. I've seen so many dead bodies now, and so many blown off arms and legs and even heads, that I wasn't even shocked. I'm afraid I've gone beyond feeling. I've slept sitting up in trenches next to mangled bodies. I've seen dead Germans and French and Americans with their eyes still open, holding letters or pictures or crucifixes. Pearl, the newspapers talk about our bravery. That's applesauce. We're always afraid, and we survive not because we're brave, but because we're numb. Numb to mud and rats and lice and bombs, and mostly numb to seeing death.

I remember the first letter I received from you here in France. You told me about the body they found in the well in Marcus. You wrote that no one knew who he was at first, and folks wondered if he had a wife, or little children, and how hard it would be for them. We see dead bodies every day, and no one thinks about whether the man had a family, or how his mother

*and father will grieve. A dead body is just
another spent shell.*

*I realize now that our training was meant not
only to prepare us to be soldiers, but to strip
away civilization. Wear the same clothes, get up
together--at all times of the night--eat what we're
told to eat, and how fast to eat it. And privacy?
Pearl, I asked Al time after time to put a lock on
the bathroom door at the barber shop. Back on
the farm, my brother and I hated to have to share
the two-holer. Now, twenty of us squat on a log
over a slit trench, and I don't give it a second
thought.*

*We learned to kill – how to shoot and where
to stab. We're not humans anymore; we're just
little cogs in a giant killing machine. I've
watched a patrol execute German prisoners in no
man's land, and I sleep just fine afterward.*

*Pearl, I'm afraid that when I come home, no
one will understand when I tell them about the
war. How can they understand? Nobody in
Cherokee's ever seen what an artillery shell does
to a human body, and no one's heard boys dying
slowly in no man's land, crying out for their
mamas. Chaplin Robb keeps a journal of every
man killed in the 168th. His journal is filling up,
Pearl, and still this war goes on.*

*Pearl, I hope that when I come home to you,
I can get back to quiet times. But I worry for
myself and all the men, that what we've seen here*

will change us forever, and I'm afraid that
returning to life as we knew it will very very hard.

With Love,

Trep.

Martin sat back and re-read the letter. Then he crumbled it and tossed it in the stove.

After only a few days' rest, the 168th was ordered to move yet again. The unit was to be on the march early in the day, and it was difficult to be up and moving with so little time off. A British liaison officer tried to move them along. "Mustn't tarry, boys. Mustn't tarry!"

For a moment Martin was back home. The trolley was about to leave, and Martin's little brother Clarence was struggling to keep up. Martin's father had timed the trip to the minute: They'd take the 5 o'clock train to Chippewa Falls, then catch the trolley for the 8 p.m. fireworks in Hallie, then leave early and take the last trolley back to Chippewa to see the fireworks from the hill at the Catholic high school "Mustn't tarry, boys!" his father shouted as they ran to the next conveyance. Finally, Clarence pleaded with his father, "Daddy, can we stop chasing the fireworks?"

Now Martin had the same thought. "Can we stop chasing the fireworks?"

On July 22nd, the unit boarded trains south of Chalons and headed to villages outside Chateau-Thierry. On the 24th, the 168th was ordered to the front, to further reduce the Marne salient and drive the wedge the Marines had opened a month earlier at

Belleau Wood to the northeast. The offensive signaled the end of trench warfare for the 168th. Over the next hundred days, Chaplain Robb would never put away his journal.

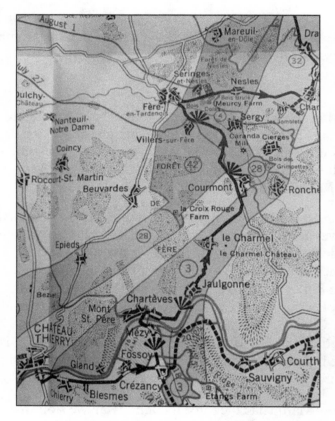

July 1918. Chateau Thierry to Nesles. "42" designates the Rainbow Division

Chapter Forty

July 26, 1918. La Croix Rouge Farm

Reserve designation was little consolation for the Third Battalion. The evening was unusually cool for late July, and the wind and intermittent showers favored no one. The men had no shelter to speak of, and long-range German artillery reached well beyond the front line. What little sleep Martin could muster was consistently interrupted by the bombardment. A Company K platoon felt fortunate to find partial refuge under one of the last remaining large trees. During the night, the tree suffered a direct hit, and six soldiers huddled beneath it were killed. The rest of the 168th dug foxholes and awaited the dawn.

The German retreat had been orderly and well-planned. There was, however, a large store of ammunition in a pocket north of Chateau Thierry. If the munitions couldn't be moved, they were to be used. As a result, the bombardment was even more fierce and frequent than usual.

Over the course of the morning, the Second Battalion was replaced in the front by the First. Martin's Third Battalion was again held in reserve. By noon, it became apparent to every private that the lines were overextended and poorly coordinated. There were gaps between 168th's right and the French infantry unit, and between the 167th Alabama on the division's left. Shortly before 3 P.M., the call went out for runners to help coordinate the front. Martin volunteered; figuring staying on the move improved his chances of not being shelled. As he delivered his message to Major Stanley, Martin looked to the northeast, where the woods ended, and the wheat fields began. He saw a group of farm buildings, perhaps 150 yards from the forest line. He also noticed colored paint splashed on the tree trunks -- white, yellow, red. Visual coordination, Martin figured, to maintain the lines once the assault began.

The buildings -La Croix Rouge farm- sat in a clearing of 3,000 acres bisected by a north south road curving southeast just below the farm. On both sides of the road were graded ditches. Martin saw the woods across the clearing; what he didn't see were German machine guns in those ditches and in the farm buildings, and artillery in the woods beyond.

Martin returned to his platoon, and the men awaited their orders. To close one gap, the Third Battalion was moved up to the left of the French unit, closer to the tree line. For several hours, the only news came in the form of wild rumors. To make matters worse, the allied artillery, which finally had gotten close enough to the front, began firing in mid-afternoon, generating a response in kind from the German guns across the clearing. Finally, near 5:00 P.M., the command was given to advance, and led by the 167th Alabama, the allies began moving toward the open field.

The farm sat atop a small rise. The first seventy-five or so yards of wheat field beyond the tree line was sloped, offering a modicum of cover. However, as soon as helmets appeared, machine guns opened up, and German field artillery let loose with deadly accuracy. The 168th's objective was the road south of the farm, and the only way to move forward was on hands and knees, and more often stomachs. No sooner had M company left the tree line when they received an order to fall back. Martin, who already was on his stomach, rolled over and crab walked slowly backwards into what was left of the forest. The ground was wet from many days' rain and the soil stuck fast to his wool uniform. His grandfather bought land with dark rich soil, beyond the reach of the last glacier. It held water as it should and made even mediocre farmers successful. The soil clinging to Martin's uniform and boots wasn't good Wisconsin loam. It was sticky clay. Martin wiped his hands on his pants and made sure the barrel of his Springfield was clean and out of the mud.

As he lay at the tree line, Martin heard the command for the 167th to move up, and he heard the rebel yell. He'd heard it back at Camp Mills, fueled by liquor and adolescent bravado. This time, though, it was borne of anger and desperation, not so much to frighten the enemy, like at Chancellorsville and Gettysburg, but more to scream away the specter of imminent death. Martin watched the Alabamans on his left advancing double quick to the farm buildings. The first wave was completely decimated by German machine guns as they crested the small rise. Survivors lay flat, yet somehow, gradually the 167th continued to forge ahead. At the same time, Company F, in the first wave of the 168th, advanced to the center, and to Martin's right, forward elements of the 29th French Infantry advanced through the open field. They, too, ran unhesitatingly to slaughter, and Martin couldn't help but wonder if any of them recited the *Te Deum* as death approached.

Eventually the 167th reached the road north of the farm and Company F drove the Germans from the ditches to the south. The farm itself was better defended. Machine gun fire continued unabated from the stone structures, and now, from across the clearing, German artillery zeroed in. Martin now realized that German artillery units, not Allied forward observers, had painted the trees. The different colors indicated distances, and Martin's Third Battalion could do nothing but pray and listen for incoming.

Finally, the remaining German gunners in the drainage ditches began abandoning their posts and retreating into the woods beyond. The Americans overran the farm buildings by nightfall, and eventually the entire clearing was taken, and the road secured.

The skies partially cleared, and forward observers saw the Germans retreating from the woods beyond the clearing. The roar of cannons was replaced by the moans and pleas of the combatants, French, American, and German. Scores more were beyond assistance.

Around midnight, great explosions were heard beyond the woods to the northeast. The Germans were speeding their retreat and destroying remaining munitions. Shortly after, the skies cleared completely, and a full moon shown on the survivors. Stretcher bearers brought in the wounded, allies and Germans alike. Martin recalled a passage from Matthew, from a long-ago confirmation class; *"He maketh his sun to rise on the evil and on the good, and sendeth rain on the just and the unjust."* He said a brief prayer for the casualties of every uniform, then closed his eyes and tried to remember a full moon enjoyed with Pearl on a warm spring Cherokee night.

Chapter Forty-One

July 27th, 1918

For the first time in days, Martin awoke to quiet voices, rather than artillery and shouting officers. French scouts had reported no German activity in the opposite woods, and much of the day was given to reorganizing the unit, moving the wounded back, and burying the dead.

In the late afternoon, orders were given to move up through the woods northeast to the Ourcq Valley. Originally, the Third Battalion was to remain in reserve, but the high number of casualties in the First led General Brown to order the Third Battalion into the line, and to connect to the 165th New York. No sooner had the march began when Martin spied a familiar face, near the head of the 165th's column, speaking to an officer he recognized as Major Bill Donovan.

"Sergeant Kilmer!" Martin yelled as his friend approached. "Why aren't you back at regiment?"

The sergeant stepped away from the officer and approached Martin. "Trep! Good to see you! I'm not 'back at regiment' because I didn't sign on to this adventure to stay behind the lines. Major Donovan's finally agreed to allow me to lead a team of scouts."

"Sergeant…"

"Joyce!"

"Okay, Joyce. You have to survive this war to tell its story. And I've been getting enough action for both of us."

"Well, you'll soon see more. The Huns have dug in on the hills above the Ourcq. You will see the ridges just after you leave these woods. Things will get hot once you move down into the valley and approach the river. The wheat fields up the hill offer little cover. It'll be a tough go, Trep. God be with you.

"And remember, you owe me dinner at Cherokee's best restaurant, Private. I'm looking forward to that."

Joyce's evaluation proved accurate; he was mistaken only in that the battalion began taking artillery fire almost immediately after emerging from the woods, as they passed La Croix Blanc Farm. The unit spread out and continued toward the Ourcq.

The Ourcq itself is barely a creek, more rivulet than river. Martin had trouble imagining that such a small stream could ever carve the wide valley into which the 168th was descending. He could see the terrain was steeper on the opposite side, but not so abrupt as to provide any meaningful cover. German machine guns and artillery were dug in on the opposite hills, and the valley provided the enemy an unobstructed view. It meant the Third Battalion's three-kilometer march to the river would be entirely within the sight and range of German artillery, and eventually their machine guns.

As they neared the Ourcq, a squad was sent ahead to determine if the Huns had destroyed the only bridge in their sector. Lieutenant Christopher returned and reported that the small span was destroyed, but the Ourcq was narrow and shallow enough for the men to easily cross. Until a temporary bridge could be erected, however, this would prove a challenge for the wagons and the artillery caissons. The point was largely academic; the men of the 168th had gotten far ahead of their mechanized support, and in light of the recent rains, it would be some time before the wagons and artillery could close ranks.

By the evening, the line of advance was no longer uniform. German artillery and machine gun fire had taken a grim toll, and there was very little allied artillery within range to soften the enemies' lines. Lacking support, the 165th New York to the right fell back, and the Third Battalion, now having its flank exposed, had no choice but to withdraw as well. M-company found itself along the river, which was fortuitous. At that point, the Ourcq is no more than six feet across and generally less than a foot deep. On both sides, however, are steep banks rising four to five feet above the running stream. The soft earth and sharp rise made it possible to quickly create rough foxholes out of the gunners' sights, and hopefully, too close to the Huns' front to draw artillery fire. It was here where Martin, hungry, mud-caked, and almost too tired to fear the threat of falling shells, huddled with his platoon through the night.

Ourcq River, looking west to Sergy. Hill 212 at right.
Photograph property of the author.

Looking up Hill 212 from the Ourcq River. *Photograph
property of the author.*

Chapter Forty-Two

*"From this day to the ending of
the world,*

*But we in it shall be remembered-
we few, we happy few, we band of
brothers; for he to-day that sheds
his blood with me*

Shall be my brother..."

> *William
> Shakespeare.
> Henry V, Act IV,
> Scene 3*

July 28th, 1918

The men of M Company were roused early, not that the intermittent bombardment and soggy conditions allowed them much rest. A white, wet fog laid a shroud over the lowest areas of the valley, but as the sun cast its first light over the ridges, the men could make out figures darting about, running ammunition down to the forward machine guns. By 6:00 A.M., all the lead companies of the Third Battalion had reached the Ourcq and were poised to assault the heights. M Company was at far left, with L Company in the center, and Company K on the right. Just as the sun reached the river bottom the command was given to advance. On his first step up the bank, Martin felt a sharp tug at his waterlogged uniform.

"Trep, I can't do it. It's too steep. I'm scared, Trep. I can't do this again."

For a second, he was thousands of miles away.

> *"Martin, I can't make it up the hill. It's too steep. My sled's too heavy and I'm tired. I can't do it."*

> *They pulled the sled up Bluff Street and crossed the railroad tracks and stood at the base of Werner's Hill. Clarence was a decade Martin's junior. Martin was annoyed at first, but then put his arm around his little brother and took the rope of his sled.*

Martin turned and faced Harry Lee, who also hailed from Cherokee. He was younger than Martin, 18 at most, and looked even younger. He was wide-eyed, and his hands were shaking.

"Harry, you can do it. It's our time to lead. You're part of M Company. We need to show those Huns what Iowa men are made of."

Martin put his arm around the young man and pulled him up the bank.

If M Company saw any good fortune that day, it was that its line of advance was directly below a small escarpment. The rise was only slightly steeper than the hillsides on the left or right, but it provided a limited measure of cover from the German forward machine guns. Several squads, including Martin's, moved quickly to the protection of this slope, and prepared to go over the top. In the midst of the maelstrom, they realized the machine gun directly in front of them was silent. The men looked over the small rise, and saw enemy soldiers frantically attending to a jammed gun. They were promptly dispatched, and Martin's platoon sprinted forward to capture the gun, and use the small earthwork as their own cover.

Two platoons of M Company were now a quarter way up Hill 212. From this vantage, they regrouped and overcame two more German machine gunners further up the hill. The forward squads now found themselves within sight of the ridge. Unfortunately, this placed them so far ahead of the allied line that they were now receiving enfilading fire from Sergy, the village to their left, and the forward machine guns to their right. The sandbags of the machine gun pits offered protection from the crest of the hill but left them completely exposed to the increasing fire from both sides. The platoons were pinned down, and all they could do was lie flat in the wheat field and hope the line would quickly move up.

Unfortunately, the other companies of the Third Battalion, and the forward battalion of the 167th, lacking the advantage of any cover, were encountering heavier fire. Their advance was considerably slower, and Martin's squad leader had already been killed. He realized something needed to be done or the both platoons would be lost. At that point, retreat was impossible, and the only hope was to get word back to the rest of the company to move up quickly. A pfc yelled to the men, "Look back down the hill. We're a goddamn nipple! And the Huns are going to pinch this nipple if we don't get somebody back to the major and tell him to get the whole damned battalion moved up. We need a volunteer!"

Martin looked around and saw wide-eyed, paralyzed with fear faces.

"One day...somewhere... you'll look and everyone around you will be shitting themselves. If you're truly a man, you'll do what they can't bring themselves to do."

"I'll do it! I'll go," Martin responded. And with that, he was up and sprinting down the hill. It was fully seventy-five yards back to the rest of the line, and Martin immediately became a tall target for enemy gunners on three sides. At first, he heard everything, nearby artillery, screams of the wounded, barked orders, and the rat-tat-tat of machine guns. Not twenty yards into his desperate sprint, however, all he heard was his own breathing. Fear was gone, and his sole focus was on his objective, now fifty, now forty yards away. At that instant, he fully understood the old gunslinger's words." *Time just slows down, and it's just you. In all the noise and commotion, you're all by yourself."*

The fields were still wet, and the clay soil grabbed at Martin's boots with every step, but he wasn't slowed, and although his breathing became heavier, adrenaline pushed him quickly onward. Now thirty yards, now fifteen, and he saw the faces of crouched comrades cheering him on. Now ten yards, now five, now just three steps to cover.

Chapter Forty-Three

Cherokee Iowa, Sunday July 28, 1918

"Miss Van de Steeg, do you have a moment?"

Maybe the popcorn machines weren't a great idea after all. Back in January, Pearl saw a machine on sale in Sioux City. She bought it and convinced the owners at the Happy Hour to install it in their theater. Shortly after, she purchased the American's machine, and Martin teased that she'd become "The Popcorn Tycoon of Cherokee County." As a pure investment, the purchases were a success; the machines paid for themselves in two months. But they needed frequent maintenance, and because trustworthy help was scarce, Pearl found herself running back and forth between the theaters on show nights to make change and collect money. And everyone wanted to rent one for their event. Pearl hadn't even gotten out of church when she was approached and asked if the boy scouts could rent the Happy Hour machine the following week for the carnival coming on Monday, the 5th. She told the fathers she'd let them know.

In fact, the popcorn machines were the last thing on her mind that afternoon. She was scheduled to play a matinee at the American. Dorothy Dutton was starring in "Flare Up Sal", billed as "A Riproaring Western!" Unfortunately, the Happy Hour had secured a special showing of "The Rainbow Division" to be shown at exactly the same time. Numerous Cherokee residents had seen the documentary in Sioux City, and believed they spotted not only some of the boys of 168th, but Cherokee's own Company M. Privately, Pearl attributed the sightings to wishful thinking, but just the same, she was not about to miss even a slim chance to see Martin. She arranged a substitute for the American, but the owner was not as understanding as she'd hoped. The fact that Flare Up Sal was a Red Cross benefit didn't help matters. She smoothed things over by agreeing to give half the American's popcorn sales to the Red Cross, but she still felt unsettled as she prepared to leave to attend the Rainbow Division matinee. The theater was full, and the piano player had brought down an extra chair for Pearl, "So you can be sure to spot Trep."

Pearl looked over the crowd as the first of the two reels began. She'd expected everyone to be excited and happy; instead, the crowd was subdued. The film was shot at Camp Mills, and the words on the screen indicated they'd just gotten the orders to ship out. By this Sunday afternoon, Cherokee had already lost several sons, and the crowd was well aware that some of the smiling boys on the big screen weren't coming home.

Pearl lost interest in trying to spot Martin. The film brought back all the sad memories of saying goodbye. The second reel concluded with shots of the *RMS Celtic*, carrying the Third Battalion of the 168th sailing past the Statue of Liberty. Pearl, however, was not in the theater to see in celluloid what she witnessed in person last fall. She'd gone home halfway through the second reel. She thought at first that a long letter to Martin would lift her spirits. But no words came. Instead, she did something she'd not done since the first day after saying goodbye to Martin in New York. Pearl allowed herself to cry.

Chapter Forty-Four

July 29, 1918. Hill 212

Private First Class Klema finished his hardtack and enjoyed his first hot coffee in four days. Several hours ago, Regimental Headquarters had given orders to prepare to advance-a directive that seemed absurd to the enlisted men, given the fact that the ridge of Hill 212 was not yet fully secured, and that Sergy, to the west, was still occupied by the Germans. The sole saving grace for Private Klema and the rest of the Third Battalion was that they were designated for reserve. Second Battalion would front the assault, with the First in support. Knowing Company M would, for the moment, be staying put, Captain Ross directed his lieutenants to collect the names of the dead and wounded. The order went down the line, and as Private Klema finished his coffee, Sergeant McManus asked to speak to him. They'd known each other before the war. McManus was a Cherokee boy; Klema was raised just up the road in Sutherland. "Bill, I need your help. I want you to contact all the platoons and get their list of dead. Get the list back to Lieutenant Christopher and make a copy for Chaplain Robb."

"One more thing. If there was anyone you know, tell Chaplain Robb you'll write the letter to the family. Can you handle this?"

"Sergeant, of course. It would be an honor."

Sergeant McManus knew the task was anything but an honor, but Private Klema had responded as expected.

It was not until the following day, however, that he was able to meet with Chaplain Robb. Although Sergy still was not completely secured, burial details had begun digging graves in a farmer's field just east of the town. It was there that Private Klema found the reverend.

"I have an incomplete list, private, and Company M casualties are mixed with I Company's. Here are the burials from this morning:

Ripple, Edward. Company I;

Hazzard, Willard. Company M;

Hammons, Henry. Company I;

Grasshoff, Henry. Company M;

Triplow, Martin. Company M."

"Triplow? Not Martin Treptow?"

"It could be Treptow. Did you know him?"

"Oh…"

Chaplain Robb saw the private catch his breath.

"He was my bunkmate when we got to France. As much as anyone can be over here, he was my best friend."

Private Klema's shoulders dropped and he let out a long sigh. The Chaplain placed Klema's hand in his and for a long moment, neither spoke.

"How?"

"I helped with the burial. It looked like artillery."

Klema said nothing for a long time, then, "He was a good man, father. I'm going to have to write to his family. He was a good man."

HILL 212 casualties, including Private Martin Treptow were buried here before being reinterred at Oise-Aisne American Military Cemetery. *Courtesy of Hubert Caloud.*

Chapter Forty-Five

Wednesday August 7, 1918

Company clerks had spent the better part of the day assembling personal effects of the dead for shipment back to the next of kin. In the late afternoon, a reporter from *Stars and Stripes* stopped by the tent to observe the process.

"Look at that pile of letters," he said. "Whose are those, corporal?"

"Whose were those?" the man replied, "They belonged to Private Treptow. That guy always got more letters than anyone else. And he seemed like he wrote back every chance he got."

"Mind if I read a couple?"

"I think what folks wrote to him were their business. I'd rather you not."

"He had a notebook, though. Actually, it looks like he had two. He talked about writing a book when he got back home. I suppose you could look at those." And he handed the reporter the two small notebooks.

The newsman paged through one of the notebooks, paused at the entry for January 1st, and read it aloud:

> *"The end of a long journey. Now bring on your 'wars'."*
>
> *1918 Resolution*

America shall win the war. Therefore,

I will work,

I will save,

I will sacrifice,

I will endure,

I will fight cheerfully and do my utmost as if the whole issue of the struggle depended on me alone."

"Holy cow. So did this Treptow guy really believe that? Did he really buy into that pledge stuff?"

"Let me tell you about Trep. He didn't buy into anything without thinking about it. You know he didn't enlist until just before the draft lottery, because he wanted to be sure in his mind we were doing the right thing. He was a barber. He probably could have stayed back at Regimental Headquarters, but he never asked. He even refused a transfer to supply. Back in the Lorraine he always took his turn on patrols, and he made sure every other man did as well. Do you read the Bible?"

"I did once. Not so much anymore."

"Trep did, and he always carried his Bible with him. I don't see it here and my guess it was on him when he died. You familiar with the Book of Hebrews?"

"I know it's in the Old Testament."

"Hebrews 13:2. *'Be not forgetful to entertain strangers: for thereby some have entertained angels unawares.'* That's the way Trep treated folks, like every stranger might be an angel in disguise."

"Here's a Trep story. Last spring, he meets some old French lady. Before you know it he's got it in his head that we need to help the locals. So no sooner does our company get off the line than he gets us all out of bed to plant potatoes!"

"Sounds like he was quite the hero."

"I don't know what a hero is anymore. We're all heroes. I know Trep wouldn't write something like that just for the sake of writing it down. That was the way he approached the war. Trep was a good man and a good soldier, and he made everyone around him a better soldier."

"So how did he die?"

"I was there. Trep's squad takes out a machine gun and moves up the hill. No sooner do they leave their cover when Corporal Grasshoff, their squad leader, takes a bullet in the forehead. Still they move up...take out a second machine gun. We're back at the river, and I could see their position's getting fire from both sides. The platoons to the right needed to move up, and I Company needed to fill the gap to their left. But with all the smoke and the noise nobody could see this, so somebody had to run back and get the word to the officers. All of a sudden what do I see but Trep hightailing it full speed down the hill. Christ almighty, I don't think Jim Thorpe ever ran faster. And by God, he almost made it. I swear he wasn't five yards from cover when a machine gun got him.

"We laid him on the ground and later someone went up and brought back Grasshoff's body. When we got orders in the afternoon to move the battalion to reserve, we saw the bodies had been hit by artillery. Grasshoff was a good soldier, too, and it was like the Huns wanted to be damn sure these guys weren't gonna come back from the dead and drive them all the way to the Rhine."

The reporter made notes and left the clerk to his duties. On August 9, 1918, a story appeared in *Stars and Stripes* describing the dangers faced by messengers during the assault on Hill 212. The article included the following:

> *On the day the Yanks went to cross the Ourcq and up the hill, Private M. A. Treptow of Iowa ran his last race from the Company to the battalion. He had almost reached his goal when a machine gun dropped him.*
>
> *Later, in the pocket of his blouse, they found his precious diary. On its first page, he had written something that many a man in this company has since copied into his own diary. It was this:*
>
> *America shall win the war; therefore I will work, I will save, I will sacrifice, I will endure, I will fight cheerfully and do my utmost, as if the whole issue of the struggle depended on me alone.*
>
> *Treptow had called this "My Pledge" and thereto he had subscribed his name.*

Chapter Forty-Six

Did you leave a wife or a sweetheart behind?

In some faithful heart is your memory enshrined?

The Green Fields of France

Eric Bogle

Saturday September 7, 1918. Cherokee, Iowa

Pearl was looking forward to a day to herself. The American Theater ran "To Hell with the Kaiser" on Wednesday, Thursday, and Friday, and each day had three showings. For the first time in as long as she could remember, she had no responsibilities for Saturday night. She planned to shop early in the afternoon, then come home and write Martin a letter. She'd been a little disappointed with his correspondence of late; she'd not received a letter since August 20th, and that was dated mid-July. She was accustomed to the thirty-day delay, but it was unlike him to not write for several weeks. She finished her home chores early and drove downtown shortly after lunch. As she walked down Main Street, she saw Al on the top step of the barber shop reading a letter. She greeted him as she approached, but Al averted her gaze.

"Pearl, Ted McCulla just brought a letter over from his son. You need to read this."

Chapter Forty-Seven

It couldn't be true. But Al's eyes, and then his tears confirmed it. The only word that came to her lips was "No." No. No! She broke away, but in that instant, Pearl was again alone in Cherokee. Main Street became foreign to her. She ran from Al, but there was nowhere to go. Not the theaters--Who is there to play for now? Not to her car. Every day for almost a year she looked at the passenger seat and imagined Martin sitting next to her.

She drove home quickly, trying not to think. After a few blocks she finally caught her breath, and then the questions overwhelmed her. What about their future…her future? What about his big homecoming? What about their trip to Paris? What about… What about their being together? And then…maybe it wasn't true. Maybe the letter was wrong. Martin couldn't be dead. They couldn't kill Trep.

Arriving at home, she saw in her mind Martin on the front steps teasing her, and then putting his strong arm around her. Tears came again and lasted through the day and into the evening. She sat down, she supported herself with a chair in the kitchen, she lay down. No position eased the pain. She closed the drapes to block the sunset and wondered if she'd enjoy a crimson end of day with anyone ever again. She went back into her bedroom and saw the vanity box, Martin's Christmas gift, on her nightstand. She cried again, then lay on the bed and let herself become numb to the world.

The theater owners came by the next morning and told her not to worry about playing for a few days. She barely acknowledged them. Louise Popma came by around noon with fresh bread and asked if she'd eaten. Pearl couldn't recall and said she had no appetite anyway. She lay down again after Louise left, not sleeping, not really awake.

She finally slept, then awoke cursing the Germans, cursing the war, cursing President Wilson, and for a blind moment, cursing Martin for leaving her.

Friends stopped by the following day. Some dared offer hope-others had been reported killed only to be found alive. Their good intentions only darkened her more. On the evening of the third day, with her tear reserves exhausted, Pearl gathered her thoughts. For almost two years her present and all of her future revolved around Martin. Now that future no longer existed. What now? Martin was Cherokee. Cherokee was Martin and Pearl. Her family had come to Cherokee when she was a young girl. She'd always felt at home here. But it would never again be the Cherokee of Martin and Pearl. Now she was a stranger, a stranger with no one to tell how she felt. Pearl's letters to Martin were more than lover's correspondence; she shared the events of her day, she shared high points and little annoyances. She shared her heart and she bared her soul. Now the anguish, the heartbreak was hers alone.

Pearl slept better the fourth night. The next morning, for the first time since she'd heard the news, she allowed herself to think of their good times. She packed a light lunch, and decided to drive to Storm Lake, to sit under the tree where she'd spent a pleasant afternoon with Martin, seemingly yesterday, but now so long ago. She'd driven only a few miles out of town and had yet to take the turn toward Aurelia when she realized it was much too soon. The empty seat next to her was Martin's. Where were his comments about the height of the corn? Where was the strong hand next to hers? Martin was everywhere, yet he couldn't be anywhere. "Why am I alone?" she thought. "Tell me God, why am I alone?"

On Saturday, September 21st, Pearl received a large envelope, addressed only to "Box 222, Cherokee, Iowa." She opened it and discovered the photograph she'd given Martin on the boardinghouse steps. Someone had read the back of the picture and sent it, as Martin directed, to his sweetheart. That night the dreams began. At first, Pearl would wake up shaking, then lie awake and cry. Eventually she began to look forward to the dreams, to talk to Martin again.

Through the rest of the fall, Pearl resolved to stay too busy to pine. She worked as many movies as time allowed, and her sister-in-law came to stay as the Christmas holidays approached. In early 1919, she traveled to Chicago to master the newest theater organs. She returned in the spring and was a featured performer at the Decoration Day services. Folks from out of town remarked that Ms. Van de Steeg gave a most impassioned solo performance that afternoon. Later that year, when Sisk and James ordered a new, ultra-modern organ for their theater, Pearl returned to Chicago to learn to play the instrument. After the organ was installed, she came back to Cherokee to perform, but after just a few weeks, Pearl returned to the Windy City, this time for good.

Chapter Forty-Eight

Thursday, September 19, 1918. Bloomer, Wisconsin

Clarence and his dad boarded the train for Eagleton and the farm, and Anna Treptow walked downtown to get the mail. She was hoping to finally receive a letter from her son. She knew from the papers that the Rainbow Division was on the move, and she expected the mail to be haphazard. It had been some time, however, since she'd received a letter from Martin. She sorted the mail from the post office box and saw nothing from her son. She was surprised, however, to receive a letter from France, with a return of "Private First-Class William Klema." She opened the letter and read:

> *Somewhere in France*
>
> *August 13, 1918*
>
> *Treptow Family, Dear Friends:*
>
> *I don't know if anyone else has written to you people or not, but Martin and I were very close friends and we often told one another that if anything ever happened to either of us, the other would write home.*
>
> *I extend to you people my most heartfelt sympathy and so do all the other boys of the company. You should be the proudest people on earth, for Martin was an ideal and a very honorable man and died the most honorable death a man can die. I know it is very, very hard*

for you but I am sure that you are brave and that you'll look at the better side. No man can do more for his country and no one can give more than you people gave.

Martin was widely known and well-liked by all. Everyone always had a glad hand or a cheerful "Hello" for "Trep" as he was usually called.

We became acquainted at Cherokee, Iowa, when he enlisted there. Last winter we were bunkmates. Martin told me so much of his home and you that I feel like I know you. He often told me, "Bill, as soon as I set foot on American soil, I'm going home." Sometimes when we are not so very well fed or when it was cold and we had no warm place to go, he would say, "Bill, I wish you and I were sitting at mother's table and feeling the heat of father's fire."

Martin was a fine soldier and not once do I know of when he was in trouble. He was killed while running with a message and nearly reached his destination. It was a very dangerous job but he did it without a murmur and seemed to be glad to be able to do such an important thing.

I know it will help you to know that he did not suffer the least as he was killed instantly by a large shell which struck right at his feet.

He is buried along the side of several other comrades. A small wooden cross is at the head of his grave which is neatly mounded up. The flowers were placed on his grave. His grave will be taken care of and if it is ever in my power I shall do all I can to make it look well.

I'm not sure just now what became of all of his personal belongings, but if you people want to know anything about him or if there is anything you would wish me to do, I will be more than pleased to help you and I want you to feel that you are not putting me out in anything you ask.

I only hope you people will look at the best side of it and be proud. It is very hard, I know, but you can have the satisfaction of knowing that your son and brother was the most honorable fellow.

Sincerely,

PRIVATE WILLIAM J. KLEMA

CO.M, 168 INF.

42ND DIV.

The following day, the family received the official announcement from the War Department.

By this time, everyone in Cherokee also had heard the news. On Monday, September 16th, the *Semi-Weekly Democrat* published an article from the Chicago Saturday Blade that included the story of Martin's pledge from the *Stars and Stripes*. Three days later, the paper published an excerpt from a letter sent from Rex Sleezer to his brother describing the assault of Hill 212. Sleezer had been wounded and wrote from a hospital near Paris. His letter confirmed that Corporal Grasshoff and Private Treptow were killed together early in the operation. Finally, on Thursday, September 26th, Al received word that Martin's sister, his life insurance beneficiary, received the formal notification from the War Department.

Chapter Forty-Nine

The trenches have vanished now under the plow
No gas, no barbed wire, no guns fire now
But here in this graveyard it's still no man's land
And the countless white crosses in mute witness stand
To man's blind indifference to his fellow man
And a whole generation who were butchered and damned
The Green Fields of France
Eric Bogle

Anna received the questionnaire just before Christmas.

For almost two years, government officials debated whether America's war dead should be repatriated. General Pershing and former President Roosevelt, who lost his own son, Quentin, argued that American soldiers were best honored by being buried where they fell. Thousands of American families thought otherwise, however, and in October 1919, the War Department sent surveys to some 80,000 families, letting them choose to have their loved ones buried in Europe, or at Arlington or some other American cemetery.

Anna wanted her son brought back to America. She debated, however, whether Martin's remains should rest at St. John's cemetery in Eagle Point, or at the city cemetery in Bloomer. By that time, the Treptows considered themselves residents of the town. Her daughter, Eleanor had married a Bloomer fellow, and the farm was now more a business than a home. On December 20th, Anna returned the questionnaire, requesting that Martin be brought to Bloomer.

On February 24, 1921, Anna accepted a certified letter from the War Department containing an instruction sheet and directions for transfer and receipt of her son's remains. The letter indicated that she'd receive a telegraph when the body arrived in the United States, and that she should immediately confirm by return telegraph the exact transfer instructions. On July 3rd, Harry Cudney called from the railroad depot, telling Anna a telegram had arrived. On the 9th, her husband Albert sent the following:

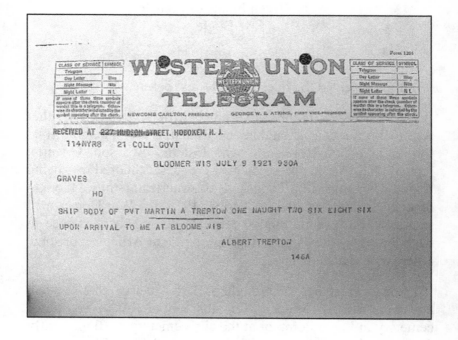

On April 29, 1921, Private Martin Treptow was disinterred from the Oise-Aisne American Military Cemetery at Seringes-et-Nesles, Plot 4, Section G, Grave No. 158. On June 19th, a ship containing his body and several hundred of his comrades left

Antwerp and docked in Hoboken on July 10th. Three years, seven months, and twenty-seven days after leaving for Europe, Trep was back on American soil.

General Pershing had agreed to meet the ships and speak at the ceremony honoring the fallen soldiers' return. On July 10th, standing on the pier with the remains of Martin and some 7000 of his comrades, the general gave a short, yet fitting tribute:

> *They gave all, and they've left us their example. It remains for us with fitting ceremonies, tenderly with our flowers and our tears, to lay them to rest on the American soil for which they died.*

Martin Treptow came home on Saturday, July 23rd, 1921. Members of the American Legion Post met his remains at the railroad depot, and accompanied the body to Werner's funeral parlor, to be placed in a proper casket for burial. The funeral was held at St. John's Lutheran Church the next day, after the regular Sunday morning service. Anna watched young war veterans and members of the ladies' aid society fill the pews. She saw the Ermatingers and the McCanns, their old Eagle Point neighbors. She hadn't expected to see so many people, folks she'd only seen at church or downtown. There were others she didn't recognize at all.

Following the service, Martin's body was borne by pallbearers and the legionnaires out of the church, and down Front Street. People were calling it Main Street by then, even though the official title still belonged to the often-flooded road along the creek. The solemn little parade moved slowly through the business district. People watched from the sidewalks, and even the teenagers outside Dettloff's soda fountain stopped what they were doing and stood quietly.

As they approached Duncan Street, Anna saw a small knot of men who stood at attention as the cortege came near. She recognized George Lane and Phillip Burke, two old Civil War veterans. Next to them were four younger men wearing dress uniforms. In April 1918, when Martin was returning to the trenches, these men were attending an enlistment party just up the street from the Treptow residence, at the home of the pretty dark eyed girl.

The city cemetery bordered the Chippewa Falls Road, at the southern edge of town. Back when Anna decided to have Martin laid to rest here, she came and walked the grounds. She saw the headstones of the city pioneers--Priddy, Van Loon, Willis-- along the high ground at its center. She circled back toward the road, to the final resting place of numerous Civil War veterans, men who purchased land with their mustering out pay, raised families, and grew old and died in Bloomer. Anna thought this little grove provided a fitting spot for her son, where the old comrades-in-arms could welcome a fellow soldier home.

Chapter Fifty

Martin was buried that afternoon with full military honors. By the next day, the neighbors had retrieved their hot dish pans, Martin's brothers had boarded the train back to Reedsburg, and Albert and Clarence had gone to the farm to attend to the birth of a new calf. The house was quiet again, and Anna's son was finally home.

On Wednesday morning, she picked a bouquet from her garden, crossed the bridge over Duncan Creek and returned to the grave. She saw new flowers, and a large wreath propped on a metal stand. The card read, "With deepest sympathy, from the Grand Army of the Republic."

Anna placed her bouquet on the grave and spotted something that made her smile- a shiny barber's shears near the headstone. Then something else caught her eye. Hidden among the flowers was what appeared to be a small branch. She picked it up and saw it wasn't a branch at all, but a tiny piece of tree root, around which was fastened a small white bow. On the bow someone had written "I sang it just for you."

Martin Treptow Memorial, Bloomer, Wisconsin *Courtesy of Hernandez Photography*

EPILOGUE

Did you really believe that this war would end wars?

But the suffering, the sorrow, the glory, the shame

The killing, the dying, it was all done in vain

...... It's all happened again

And again and again and again and again....

The Green Fields of France

Eric Bogle

Bernard took the tractor out of gear, reached in his pocket for the small silver case and lit his last cigarette. He was down to three a day and this would be his reward for finishing the 20 hectares. The weather held, and he'd gotten the last of the seeds in with no stalls and no mud clogs. He gazed across the wide valley into the setting sun. Maybe half the fields were planted, and other tractors were working the spring ground.

He'd leased the field since 2005. His father held the tenancy for the previous 59 years, and before that his grandfather had toiled on the land for the owner. For at least a century the field had yielded fine wheat, but the family adapted to change after the second war, when an international market developed for rapeseed. At first, it was used chiefly as a lubricant; later, as Europe and the United States became health conscious, it became more valuable in its refined state, as canola oil. Crop prices had risen steadily for two decades, enabling Bernard to purchase some of the newest and best tools of his trade.

Bernard was at the helm of a new John Deere row crop tractor. His planter was a twelve row with a laser system that would transform the uneven hillside into perfect undulating waves of yellow come mid-summer. The comfortable cab was nothing like what he grown up driving, but still, after a long day in the field, he was ready for a hot bath and a good dinner.

The crest of the hill provided an unobstructed view for miles, down to the Ourcq River, the southern boundary of his field, into the village of Sergy and when the lights of the city came on, to Fere en Tardenois, ten kilometers to the northwest. Over the entire field, there were only two small slopes, one directly below the other, where he couldn't confirm if his planting had been absolutely uniform.

Bernard grew up in Soissons, to parents who remembered the occupation as little children, and whose fathers had fought the Boche in *la Grande Guerre*. His father's father hated the Germans to the end of his days. His parents' feelings were less strong, and to Bernard, *Allemagne* was simply another market for his product.

He'd not forgotten his grandparents' stories, however. Bernard knew that in the hills to the southwest lay the ruins of La Croix Rouge Farm, where Americans from the states of Iowa and Alabama fought and died in the summer of 1918. He knew the small eminence on which he was enjoying his cigarette was "Hill 212", even though his onboard GPS told him the elevation was closer to 210. Every spring, the plows would turn up reminders of that century old carnage. The farmers called it *"recolte de fer"*- the iron harvest

Bernard finished his smoke and turned the tractor to the road along the east ridge. Just down to the northeast was the Oise-Aisne American Cemetery, the perpetual resting place of the young men who'd stormed the hill a hundred years earlier.

As he turned the wheel, the setting sun highlighted the inscription on the silver cigarette case. Until a month ago, the case rested above his fireplace. It was a long-ago gift from his grandfather, who told Bernard he'd found the little case and pages of a Bible on the hill he'd just planted – shortly after the first war. Bernard kept candy in it as a youngster, then forgot about it for decades until his wife retrieved it from the mantle and cleaned it, pleased that it could hold only a limited number of cigarettes and a small lighter.

In all the years Bernard owned the case, he'd paid no attention to the inscription. His grandfather said it was a famous quote by *de Fontenelle*, but the words held no interest for the young man, and years of tarnish obscured the phrase until his wife had the little compact restored.

He rotated the case to read the full inscription and gazed again over the old battlefield. The words read,

"Qu'est-ce que l'historie, mais une fable convenue?

What is history, but a fable agreed upon?

CURTAIN CALL...INTRODUCING THE CAST...

There are very few fictional characters in this book. Several have been subjects of their own books, and a few more would be good candidates. Assuming I got the dates and places correct, most everything I describe in the book really could have happened. Now let's meet the cast, roughly in order of their appearance.

JOSEPHINE GAUTHIER ROBERT

Josie would be a fine candidate for a book of her own. Shortly before World War I, the *Eau Claire* [Wisconsin] *Leader* ran a series of short biographies highlighting the lives of Chippewa Valley pioneers. Included was a story written by Josephine Robert herself. She really did speak three languages, she really did master the river at a very early age, and she probably knew Jean Brunet as well as anyone. Another article told about a trip up the Chippewa River shortly after the Civil War. The young travelers described the hospitality of Brunet's trading post, and the intelligence and beauty of Francois Gauthier's daughter. Josie and her husband eventually moved from the land she'd inherited from Jean Brunet, and built a home outside Holcombe, Wisconsin. She lived a long, full life. I'll bet she was quite a woman.

JEAN BRUNET

Here's another character who merits a book of his own. Brunet was born in France, and traveled to what was then the western frontier, Fort Crawford, near present day Prairie du Chien. He served in the state militia and the territorial legislature. He also ran a shipping business and learned the waterways of the territory. He was hired to build a sawmill at the falls of the Chippewa River, just north of the clear tributary the French called *l'eau Claire*. The enterprise failed, but he had no appetite to head back downriver. Brunet and his assistant, Francois Gauthier built a cabin just below one of the lesser falls to the north. Due to good fortune or good hospitality, or both, it became a favored stopping point for river travelers and anyone traversing the old Indian trail west of the river.

Brunet's historical footprint straddles two significant periods in the history of the Wisconsin Territory and early statehood. At Prairie du Chien, he certainly was familiar with, and likely profited from, the Upper Mississippi fur trade. Just as the business was sunsetting in the late 1830's, Brunet was hired by Lyman Warren, a son-in-law of the famous fur trader Michel Cadotte, to head upriver and plant the seeds of a new enterprise, one that would dominate the upper Midwest for the next six decades

Jean Brunet is buried in Chippewa Falls, and Brunet Island State Park, located a mile upriver from the old trading post, bears his name.

THE TREPTOW FAMILY

Martin Treptow, for whom his grandson was named, emigrated from Germany shortly before the Franco-Prussian War. He settled in Kenosha, and saved enough money to purchase farmland in southern Chippewa County. There's a rough rectangle of land bordered by the Chippewa River on the east, Chippewa Falls to the south, and rolling hills to the north and west. The land is immediately below the southern fingerprint of the last glacier and features some of the most productive farms in that part of the state. Martin Treptow's 80 acres fell within that rectangle.

Grandpa Treptow died in an accident soon after the family moved, and his son, Albert maintained the farm and raised a family. Shortly after the turn of the century, he decided to move to the "city" of Bloomer, population all of maybe 1,000. The farm must have been reasonably successful, because the family could afford to build a new home and still keep the business. Both properties stayed in the family name until the 1940s, and there still are old-timers in the Chippewa Falls area who remember Albert.

Clarence Treptow, Martin's youngest brother, lived in Bloomer his entire life, and passed away in 1978 at the age of 73. When I was a boy, Clarence was the friendly old guy who cleaned up around the city parks and mowed the little league fields. He had a smile for everyone, and exhibited, in more reserved fashion, the genuine good nature that so many folks saw in his older brother.

FREDERICK WEYERHAEUSER

Mr. Weyerhaeuser was a German born Illinois businessman. In the 1870s, he cobbled money together and purchased a failing logging company based at the mouth of the Chippewa River. The operation was successful, and he later purchased a majority interest in the Chippewa Lumber and Boom Company, and eventually controlled most the lumber business on the lower Chippewa. At one time, the sawmill below the Chippewa falls was the largest operation of its kind under one roof in the entire world. By the early 20th century, after having denuded immense tracts of forest land and after transferring his operation to the Pacific Northwest, Frederick Weyerhaeuser was one of America's richest men.

FRANK ERMATINGER & MICHEL CADOTTE

Jean Brunet didn't operate the only trading post on the Chippewa River. Years earlier, Michel Cadotte, a fur trader and entrepreneur known throughout the upper Great Lakes, came south from Lake Superior with his wife Equaysayway and traded pelts with the Ojibwe near the Yellow River. Their first child was born there. Another trading post, located at Vermillion Rapids, roughly midway between the Chippewa falls and where Brunet would build, was run by James Ermatinger. Ermatinger married a daughter of Michel Cadotte, following the death of Truman Warren, the brother of Jean Brunet's financier.

The village of Jim Falls, located near the old trading post, is named after Mr. Ermatinger, and Cadott, on the Yellow River, bears the anglicized name of that other early pioneer.

When Equaysayway was baptized into the Catholic faith, she was given the name Madeline. Her father, a well-regarded Ojibwe chief, decreed that the large island in Chequamegon Bay would henceforth forever bear her name.

JOSEPH DUGAL

Joseph Dugal also was a real person, but his story is short. He was killed when his head was crushed by a replacement beam on one of the new bridges over the Chippewa River. The reporter actually described the condition of his head as a "shapeless mass." Now that's what you call writing.

OLE HORNE (SOMETIMES SPELLED HORAN) AND THE LOGGING DISASTER

There really was a logging disaster on July 7, 1905, in which 11 men, including the famous "Whitewater Ole" lost their lives. Late on Thursday, July 6th, a log jam developed below the Little Falls Dam, near Holcombe. A call went out to Chippewa Lumber headquarters, and early the next morning several dozen eager, but probably still tipsy or at least hung-over lumberjacks hopped on the train from Chippewa Falls. They proceeded to overload a bateau and failed to secure both ends of the boat when they reached the jam. The boat swung sharply in the current, and almost everyone went into the water, around or under the logs. Ole Horne, who, it was said, could dance on a rolling log, was the last to be found, not far from his home on the river. He's buried in Chippewa Falls.

THE PRETTY, DARK-EYED TEENAGE GIRL

Bluff Street in Bloomer is now 19th Avenue, and the bluff across the railroad tracks, called Werner's Hill at the turn of the century, sports luxury homes. If Martin took Clarence sledding, they'd have walked up Bluff Street, and they really would have passed the home of a pretty, dark-eyed teenage girl. She was a couple years Martin's junior, and her name was Veronica Sleeter. She remembered Martin in her later years. I know this because Veronica Sleeter was my great aunt. Judging from the old pictures, I think "pretty, dark-eyed teenage girl' describes her quite well.

GUS

I don't give him a last name in the book, but many readers will quickly figure out that I'm referring to Gus Dorais. Charles "Gus" Dorais was raised in Chippewa Falls, and after being turned down by the University of Minnesota, went to play quarterback for what was then a small, nondescript Catholic college in Indiana. Contrary to myth, Gus Dorais did not throw the first forward pass, but certainly the Gus Dorais to Knute Rockne passing combination revolutionized the game. Gus Dorais also served during the First World War. Afterward, he coached and mentored young men for decades. Several books have been written about Gus Dorais, the most recent being *Gus Dorais*, by Joe Niese. It's an entertaining and informative read.

JOHN COOK

Johnny Cook, the Cameron boy who beat Gus in a race on Rice Lake, joined the service in World War I and survived the sinking of the *Tuscania*. I can't say if Johnny and Gus actually worked on the railroad together, or if they raced each other in Rice Lake. I think it's fair to say, though, that Mr. Cook likely was a pretty good swimmer.

FRANK DOLAZEL

Contemporary Marshfield newspapers always had good things to say about Frank Dolazel. He'd spent time in the Dakotas and was by all accounts a renowned raconteur. His barber shop was well located near the railroad depot and from what I can gather, everyone in town knew and liked him. If the man who cut the hair and provided the shave got the money, the lion's share of the shop's take probably went to Frank.

COLE YOUNGER

Cole Younger, was a member of the James Gang. He was shot to pieces during the Northfield raid, captured, and served time in prison. After his release, he traveled with Buffalo Bill's Wild West show and later lectured around the country on his own. In mid-April 1911, Cole Younger gave a lecture in Cherokee, Iowa entitled "What Life Has Taught Me." He also spoke throughout Wisconsin, and traveling from Wausau to Eau Claire, would have passed through Marshfield by train.

Martin and Cole's meeting, while chronologically plausible, is, of course, just my way of getting Martin to Cherokee. There's a fair amount of biographical material out there, and there are Treptows living in northwest Iowa to this day. While they enjoy sharing the surname, they do not believe there is, or was, any blood relation. I suspect this has more to do with the passage of time than any real certainty. Anyway, lacking a provable family connection, I invited Mr. Younger to make a cameo appearance.

WILSON McDANIEL, THE BARBER SHOP ROBBER

Just before Martin arrived in Cherokee, Wilson McDaniel, an employee of Al Popma's brother stole money and barber tools and jumped on the train to Sioux City. He was captured exiting the train. Who better than Martin to trip him up?

AL POPMA

Al Popma was born in 1885, and according to newspaper articles, began barbering at the tender age of 12. He started at Cherokee in 1911, along with his cousin, Walter. He continued in the trade for another 70 years.

Newspaper articles written when he was close to retirement portray him as a friendly, God-fearing workaholic. Contemporary newspapers characterized him as a hard worker with a big heart and a giant dollop of civic pride. If Cherokee ever gets the book it deserves, Al Popma merits at least a chapter.

PEARL VAN DE STEEG (sometimes spelled Van de Steig)

Pearl fascinated me from the first time I met her in the old Cherokee newspapers. She was a local star. She somehow talked the owners of the Happy Hour and American to allow her to play at both theaters, and only for the best, most popular pictures. When an Easter pageant required someone to sing the grand finale, when a picnic needed a singer, they called Pearl. She also produced concerts and plays.

She was an independent businesswoman. In the mid-year 1915 census, she reported her age as 24, rather than 22, and bought a house. She traveled to Des Moines and Chicago to train on the newest organs, and she ultimately owned the popcorn machines in both the American and Happy Hour Theaters. There is a comment in Martin's writings referring to being in the roadster with Pearl. I found nothing indicating that Martin owned a car and a reasonable assumption is that Pearl, a young single woman in 1917, owned her own vehicle. A "roadster" probably would have been one of the new Dodge Brothers cars, and in fact, Cherokee had an early Dodge Brothers dealership. Remember, this was at a time when folks were still getting used to women wearing bloomers and riding bicycles.

Maybe most impressive is the fact that when Martin was stationed at Camp Mills, New York, Pearl took a leave of absence from her jobs and all by herself, traveled east and rented an apartment in New York City.

There's no question that Pearl and Martin were deeply in love. He mentions her often in his writings, and his journal entries reflect the significant number of letters they exchanged while he was in Europe. After Martin passed away, Pearl moved to Chicago and married, and became--as anyone in Cherokee would have expected--a successful businesswoman. Ultimately, she retired with her husband and spent the rest of her days in Florida. She passed away in July 1974. Among her personal effects was an old photograph of Pearl with a handsome young soldier. On the back it read, "In case of accident, please send this picture to my sweetheart, Box 222, Cherokee, Iowa."

When someone writes that Cherokee book, Pearl gets a chapter, too.

EVERETT McMANUS

Judging from Martin's letters and his journal, Sergeant Everett McManus was a good friend. He's mentioned often in the journal entries. Martin's war story ended on July 28, 1918, but the American Expeditionary Force's war didn't wind down, it ramped up. From August 1st until the November 11th Armistice, the United States suffered more casualties per day than in any other war, before or since. Think about that.

Sergeant McManus was killed by machine gun fire on September 12, 1918.

BILL KLEMA

Bill Klema grew up in Sutherland, Iowa. Martin met Bill during their first encampment, at the Iowa State Fairgrounds. It doesn't appear that they were in the same platoon, but Martin's journal and Bill's letters indicate they remained friends in France and were bunkmates for a time. Bill's letter to Martin's parents is reprinted in exact form.

ALFRED JOYCE KILMER

Joyce Kilmer was one of America's most well-known poets at the beginning of the 20th century. Joyce and his wife had five children, and when one contracted polio shortly after birth, they converted to Catholicism. Joyce joined the service immediately after war was declared, but it took some time to convince his superiors that he wished to be more than a recruiting poster boy. He turned down an officer's commission at least once, and in April 1918, was allowed to join his unit at the front. On July 30, 1918, Major Bill Donovan ("Wild Bill" later of OSS fame) invited him to join a forward observation squad near Meurcy Farm, on the other side of the hill from where Martin lost his life two days earlier. Joyce Kilmer was killed by a sniper on July 30th. He is buried at the Oise-Aisne American Cemetery near Fere en Tardenois.

Martin's friendship with Joyce is, of course, fictitious but it's a virtual certainty that, given Kilmer's fame, Martin would at least have known who he was, and quite possibly, met him, either at Camp Mills or in France. Interestingly, the same day Martin was being discharged from the hospital; Sergeant Kilmer was accompanying wounded men from his unit back to the same hospital.

THE TALKATIVE WAITER AT THE RITZ

I had great fun with Martin's trip to Paris, and dinner at the Ritz. There actually was a gap in time between Martin's discharge from the hospital and his orders to report back to his unit. He filled the time by working at a supply depot on the outskirts of Paris, and likely would have visited the city. At the same time, Joyce Kilmer had submitted the poem *Rouge*

Bouquet for publication. It was hardly the uplifting saga of bravery that his publicist hoped for; it detailed the death of 19 of his comrades.

In 1918, the Ritz was one of Paris' newer luxury hotels, although like other fine establishments, it would have been short staffed because of the war. To fill the need, young men from Indochina--called Anamese--were frequently employed at Paris restaurants, including the Ritz. One hire was an outspoken young man who had left his hometown of Hanoi to travel the world by ship. He worked for a time at the Parker House in Boston and learned passible English. He then traveled to France and worked at the Ritz during the war. After the Armistice, he managed to get himself physically thrown out of the Versailles peace talks, after which he returned to his home country. He remained politically active throughout his life, eventually changing his name to one with which Americans will be more familiar: Ho Chi Minh.

THE SCOTTISH HIGHLANDER

I've taken some liberties with several characters described in Martin's journals. One was a broad-shouldered Scotsman who preferred kilts to a regulation uniform, and who apparently was not attached to any identifiable unit.

BOB REED AND LOUIE WEISS

The 168th's Chaplain, Winfred Robb maintained a journal during the war, consisting of short biographical sketches of soldiers killed in combat. Privates Reed and Weiss were two who found their way into Chaplain Robb's journal. Private Reed's bravery and stoicism, despite being mortally wounded, was mentioned not only by Chaplain Robb but in the official regimental history.

THE BLOOMER VETERANS

I describe a handful of Bloomer veterans who watched as Martin's body was borne from St. John's Lutheran Church through the main business section, to the city cemetery. By that time, many of Bloomer's Civil War veterans had passed away, but at least two, George Lane and Phillip Burke, were still alive, and active in the Grand Army of the Republic. The "four younger veterans" were men who posed with small U.S. flags at an April 1918 going away party, just up the street from the Treptow residence. The four, Louis Kranzfelder, Jack Klund, Leonard Loehnis, and Oscar Nelson were fortunate enough to survive the war and return home. Louie Kranzfelder was my great uncle, and I wish I'd had the wisdom as a youth to ask him about his experiences.

MARTIN TREPTOW

The fact that I have more to say about him means I probably didn't describe him well enough in the book. I've read the available biographical information, his journals, his letters, and comments and stories written about him at the time. He had a heckuva knack for making people like him. He was friendly, funny, outgoing and always willing to lend a hand. He exhibited exceptional intellectual curiosity; he asked questions, and he was remarkably well-read. His writing was grammatically correct, and his vocabulary belied his paucity of formal education. His handwriting was calligraphic.

I intentionally left the exact circumstances of Martin's death unclear. Was he killed by machine gun fire, or artillery? The earliest reports, Chaplain Robb's, and the *Stars and Stripes* article, contradict each other. I've visited the battlefield several times, and I've reviewed regimental maps and the official history. A theory that makes sense to me was posited by Darrek Orwig, an experienced 168th Infantry researcher, and the author of *Somewhere Over There, The Letters, Diary and Artwork of a WW1 Corporal.* He suggests that if Martin was killed by machine gun fire early in the assault, his body would have been left on the field. As the 168th moved up the hill, German field artillery would have become less concerned about dropping friendly fire. If the bodies were hit by shells, Chaplain Robb, coming by the next day with a burial detail, might reasonably have concluded that Martin was killed by artillery.

Martin Treptow achieved minor fame in the months after he passed away, when part of his pledge appeared on a poster for the newest Liberty Bond Drive. He found posthumous fame again in 1981, when his name was mentioned (although mispronounced), and his pledge recited by President Reagan during his first inaugural address.

I think it misses the point to idolize Martin Treptow simply because of his pledge. The pledge was one of dozens of lofty promises to which all Americans, young and old, military and civilian, were asked to ascribe to during the war. It's entirely possible that Martin merely paraphrased something he heard or read. What makes Martin Treptow special is not that he wrote a pledge, it's that, by all accounts, he truly believed in what he was writing, and he lived the words.

Martin was a brave soldier. He turned down at least one opportunity to be transferred away from the front, and he regularly volunteered for scout patrols, dangerous night missions in no man's land. However, Martin Treptow probably was no more a hero than a hundred thousand other American doughboys. But the way he framed his commitment to service through his pledge embodies the indomitable spirit of the American soldier, not only in the First World War, but in every war and conflict in which the American military has honorably served.

I have no doubt that Martin began his second journal with a book in mind. Had he returned home, that book would've been funny and serious and thoughtful and very well written. It would've told of the bravery of his comrades. But I don't think he would've said much about Martin Treptow. I hope I have.

CPSIA information can be obtained
at www.ICGtesting.com
Printed in the USA
LVHW111317021220
673214LV00005B/242

9 781647 190392